~~~~~~~~~~~~~~~~~~~~~~~~~~~~~~~~~~~

Mystery in the Attic

~~~~~

By Pamela Clayfield

~~~~~~~~~~~~~~~~~~~~~~~~~~~~~~~~~

Mystery in the Attic
by Pamela Clayfield

Copyright © 2008

Online editions may also be available for this title.

Previously titled Love... Pure & Simple

ISBN: 978-1-257-93326-6

To anyone who has ever been in love... pure & simple.

CHAPTER 1

Lisa tucked a stray strand of red hair behind her ear and tried desperately to focus on the financial plan that was before her. She'd promised these customers she'd have an Investment Portfolio proposal prepared for them by the end of the week. They had inherited a large sum of money and wanted it invested in 'all the right places' she'd been told. So she had begun working at lining up the best options for them but they weren't willing to go high-risk with their money so that left her at a disadvantage because there were limited options otherwise. She ran her fingers through her layered waves and sighed heavy as she pushed herself away from her desk and stood.

"Tough day?" Steve asked as he walked by.

"You don't know the half of it," she replied. "I'm going to get a drink."

"Rum perhaps?" Steve joked.

"Yeah, straight up, maybe a twist of lime but I don't want to dilute it too much," she replied.

Steve laughed and nodded. "The joys of financial planning."

Lisa nodded and went to the staff room where she grabbed a new bottle of water from the fridge and struggled to get it open before she slumped down onto the couch and put her head back willing the tears not to come. *Not yet, just not yet*, she thought and closed her eyes to keep from crying. She fought once more with the lid on the water bottle and this time she got it open. She drank about half of it before she pushed herself off the couch and went back to her office.

"I hate to interrupt," a small voice said from her doorway just as she was sitting down.

"What is it?" she asked.

"I need verification for this cheque, it's over my limit," one of the tellers explained.

Lisa smiled and motioned for her to come to her desk. She listened to what the teller had to say and then put her initials on the cheque. She turned her attention back to the mess before her but was grateful when another of the tellers tapped on her door and told her she had a customer looking to apply for a line of credit.

"I'll be right with them," Lisa said and watched as the teller walked away to talk to the customer. She took a deep breath. *I can't do this anymore,* she thought as she stood and straightened her skirt before she rounded her desk and left her office.

An hour later she was shaking hands with the customers she'd just finished helping. The application was in for their line of credit.

"I'll call you when I get the answer," she told them. She turned to look at the clock and realized it was time to go home. *Thank God,* she thought as she went back into her office to put things away.

"Can I have a word?" Gerry asked.

Lisa looked up at her branch manager and nodded. "I'll be there in a sec," she said. She was going to get her purse so she could leave as soon as she was finished.

A few minutes later she was tapping on Gerry's door.

"Come in, sit down," he said waving at one of the two chairs before his desk.

Lisa sat down and set her purse at her feet.

"I noticed you didn't take any vacation time this summer," Gerry pointed out.

Lisa opened her mouth to say something but was abruptly cut off.

"I've also noticed you seem to be stretched to your max," he went on.

Lisa nodded. "I, well..." she said and then the tears came. As much as she willed them not to, they poured down her cheeks and she was no longer able to stop them.

Gerry stood, picked up his box of tissues and rounded the desk to sit in the chair next to her. He extended the box towards her and waited for her to take one. "Listen, this isn't an easy job and you are great at what you do. I don't want to lose you."

Lisa sobbed a little harder. She had heard at one time that getting a compliment out of this particular branch manager was a difficult feat at best and here she was being praised for sitting in his office bawling and she smiled inwardly at the irony of it all. "I need to take time off," she told him. "I know I do. I've been feeling it building for a while," she said sniffing between each sentence. "I just never seem to find a point where everything is wrapped up and I could get away."

"That time is going to be now," Gerry told her. "Whatever you have left to do, I want you to pass it off to Steve or Julie tomorrow and then you're gone. You get four weeks and I think you should take all of it."

Lisa nodded. Not exactly something she was proud of but she was still sure it was what she wanted to do. She picked up her purse. "Thank you, Gerry," she said quietly.

"Don't mention it, just take a break, get some rest and take some time to get away," he told her. "It will do you a world of good."

Lisa stood and left his office. She was glad she'd grabbed her purse first as she could walk out the door and not have to face her co-workers. She walked quickly to her car and drove the short distance to her apartment. She was still blowing her nose and she slipped inside unseen. She stripped out of her work clothes and fell onto the bed. She took several deep breaths. She had one more day of work to go and then she was on vacation for a month. *What am I going to do for a month?* She wondered and shrugged her shoulders. She got up and wandered to the kitchen to make herself some supper when the phone rang.

"Hello?" she answered even though call display told her it was her mother and she sucked in a breath to brace herself.

"Hi, it's me," her mother began.

"Hello," Lisa said again used to the ritual. "What's up?" She propped the phone between her ear and her shoulder and filled a pot with water.

"Not much, called to say hi. What are you doing?" her mother asked.

"Just making some supper," Lisa told her.

"I wanted to know what you're doing for Thanksgiving."

Now Lisa sucked in a deeper breath. How was she going to say this. "I don't know mom," she replied.

"What do you mean you don't know? I'm having dinner, as always," Molly told her.

"I might not be in town mom," Lisa told her.

"Oh?"

"I'm taking the next four weeks off work, Gerry's forced the issue and I'm finally doing it. And I really need to get away," she said feeling like she was pleading her case. Never mind that she was almost 30 years old and it was her choice.

"Where will you go?"

"I'm not sure yet but I was thinking of heading towards one of the lakes or something, maybe stay at some B&Bs and see what I can find. Maybe I'll even write a book," she replied.

Finally her mother laughed. "Maybe you'll meet a boy," she said.

Lisa wanted to scream. Every time, every single time they talked her mother brought this up. "Well for one thing mom, I'm looking for a man, not a boy," she corrected.

"Whatever. At least someone who is husband material, and has some sperm."

"MOM!"

"Well, I want to have more grandkids, is that horrible?"

"No, but do you irritate Kelly and Steven this way?" referring to her siblings. "No, you don't."

"But your sister *is* married and has a little one and Steven is, well he's a boy. It's different for boys," Molly retorted.

Lisa had had enough of this particular conversation. "I'm going to do some poking around online tonight and see what I can come up with for some time away. If I don't find something for the long weekend, I'll come for dinner."

Her mother seemed satisfied with this answer and they said goodbye shortly after.

Lisa sat and put her head in her hands. *I just can't go on like this,* she told herself. *It's time. I will not be around for Thanksgiving dinner. Or the entire weekend for that matter.*

She ate supper alone while she made a list of what projects at work she needed to hand over to Steve and Julie. She didn't have too much at that point, mostly just a review of her existing customer's portfolios and that would have to wait until she got back. When she'd put her dishes away, she settled down in front of the computer and typed *accommodations* into her search engine and ended up at a site for *Accommodations in Canada* where she could pick and choose from various parts of the country and then the province. She clicked on several of them and finally came across two she really wanted to visit and wrote down the names, addresses and phone numbers so she could call them and book when she decided she would be leaving which she had a feeling would be on Saturday.

Satisfied she'd accomplished what she could, she climbed into bed and turned on the TV in her room just to take a break from reality when the phone rang again.

"Hello?" she asked, this time not bothering to look at the call display.

"It's me again dear," her mother's voice came through the line.

"What now?" Lisa asked trying desperately to hold on to what remained of her patience.

"I was wondering what you'll do about the choir," Molly replied.

"I'm telling them I'm going to be away, period. It's none of their business that I need some time away. *I need a break*," she said emphasizing the last four words.

"Okay, I was just asking, wanted to make sure you didn't just disappear on them."

They hung up a moment later and Lisa growled at the phone. She was so tired of the demands placed on her at home, at work and at church. *If I don't get away from here soon I think I'm going to self-combust.*

She turned off the movie, no longer in the mood to watch it and then turned out the light. She cried in the darkness, tears of frustration and anger and even some of depression and lonliness. Eventually she fell asleep but it didn't give her the rest she needed.

CHAPTER 2

Lisa woke the next morning and felt awful. She didn't know how she'd get through the day but hope sprang eternal when she remembered the phone calls she would be making to the B&B's to see about getting a room. She hoped they didn't close completely for the fall and winter months. She was pretty sure they didn't, or at least most of them anyway, and was confident she would get a room at one of them. She was hoping to get into the one on the lake first in order to be able to take some time watching the sunset before it was too cold to do so.

She got in the shower and just stood there letting the hot water pour over her. As she was drying off, she wondered if she'd actually used soap as she had done it strictly out of habit.

Her hands shook as she readied herself for work, choosing carefully what she would wear. She wasn't sure why, perhaps it was to leave a lasting impression on Gerry so she really would still have her job in a month from now.

A little while later she settled herself at her desk and turned on her computer. She pulled out her list and began to itemize everything so nothing would be forgotten. She checked her planner when her computer came up and wasn't surprised that she had forgotten a few of the accounts.

She looked at the clock and wondered if it was too early to make a few phone calls and decided that if it was a Bed and Breakfast she was calling then it probably wasn't too early. She figured she'd do this now because if she didn't, she wouldn't be going anywhere the following day.

She got through to the first place she wanted to stay on and her call was answered on the first ring which threw her a little. Uh, yes, I, um, sorry, I wasn't expecting someone to answer quite so quickly," she explained.

"That's okay, I wasn't really expecting the phone to ring but I happen to be sitting right next to it." The male voice at the other end sounded inviting and Lisa was surprised at how drawn she was to it.

"I'd like to know if you have any rooms available, it's kind of short notice," she said.

"How short of notice are you giving me? You're not on your way now are you?" the man asked.

"No, of course not, no," she stammered. "But I was thinking of tomorrow," she told him and waited with bated breath.

"Tomorrow is fine. Today would be fine too actually," came the reply.

"I'm working today, I'll be leaving tomorrow morning," she confirmed.

"How many nights will that be?" he asked.

"Oh, right, um, I was thinking two, maybe three at the most," she replied. *Boy, I really have my head screwed on straight don't I?* she thought.

"I'll put you down for three and if you leave early it won't harm anything, if you decide to stay it won't either, it's not exactly the time of year I get a lot of reservations," he explained.

"I'm sure you don't, well, I'll see you tomorrow," she said as she saw more of the staff starting to come in.

"That's great, oh, what's your name?"

"Oh, right, it's Lisa, Lisa *Davies*," she replied.

"I'll see you tomorrow Lisa, goodbye for now."

She set the phone in the cradle just in time to wave to Steve as he went by.

"I'll need a few minutes later on so pencil me in," she called to him.

"Sure thing," he replied with a returned wave.

She saw that everyone had settled into their offices so she picked up the phone and called the second B&B on her list and went through a similar routine with them, however they were far more formal than the first and she was surprised at how intrigued she was by the man she would be meeting tomorrow. It always struck her how those things seemed to happen. She had developed quite an intuition and though she didn't qualify herself as a psychic, she knew she certainly had that *sixth sense* that would drive it if she ever chose to develop that.

She saw Julie come in and was a little surprised when she stopped outside the door and wished her a good morning.

"Good morning," Lisa replied tentatively.

"I need to run something by you later on," Julie told her.

"Okay, actually that works because I need to do the same with you," Lisa told her not wishing to get into why right now.

"Okay great, let me get settled and then maybe we can get started," she said as she walked toward the staff room.

Lisa shook her head. Julie was not one of her favourite co-workers. She was rude and wanted to make her way to the top no matter who she hurt or stabbed in the back on the way up the corporate ladder. She wondered what it was that Julie needed from her but felt an odd sense of satisfaction about telling her that she was leaving for a month.

"I have about fifteen minutes right about now," Steve said from her doorway surprising her.

"Okay, great, have a seat," Lisa told him pointing at one of her chairs. As she looked through her door, she saw that Julie was walking away a little disappointed that she had to wait to speak with her and she smiled inwardly.

"So what's up?" Steve asked her.

"I'm leaving for a month and I need you to take over some of my portfolios for a while when I'm gone."

"Is everything alright?" he asked looking concerned.

"Yes, well, no, I'm just in desperate need of some time away. I'm really feeling stressed out and feel the need to run away for a while."

"Sure, I'll do whatever you need me to do," he assured her and borrowed a pen and pad so he could take notes.

It was almost half an hour later when he left her office with an armload of files. "'Cause I didn't have enough to do already," he joked.

"I'm sorry," Lisa said feeling a little guilty.

Steve stopped and stuck his head back in her door, "*don't* be sorry," he told her.

She nodded and again had to fight off the tears.

She was relieved though because she had just passed off the difficult customer file she'd been working on the day before. Steve was more advanced than she was so maybe he would find it easier to invest the way they wanted it. Just as she was about to turn her attention to one of the smaller projects she wanted to finish before she left, Julie appeared in her doorway.

"Can *I* see you now?" Julie asked.

Lisa could tell right away that Julie was at least a little perturbed that Lisa had been busy with Steve when she wanted a few minutes. "Yeah, come in," Lisa said offering the same seat Steve had just left.

Julie sat down and set a file on the desk in front of her.

"So what's up?" Lisa asked eyeing the folder.

"I was wondering if you could take this, I think you'd be better able to help these people than I can," Julie said as she pushed the file across the desk.

Lisa didn't even look at it. "I can't, I actually needed to see you because I'm going away for a month and I need you to take on a number of my customers," Lisa told her.

"Oh, um, okay, I guess I'll ask Steve to take it," Julie replied.

Lisa didn't tell her that she'd just finished handing over even more of her workload to Steve, she thought it would be interesting to see what happened after she'd paid Steve a visit. "What was wrong with that file?" she asked more out of curiosity than anything else.

"Well, uh, I just, don't worry about it, I'll see if Steve can take it," Julie said.

Lisa nodded and turned towards her computer while Julie walked towards Steve's office and then she smiled. Julie was like that, if she just didn't want to take on a portfolio she tried dumping it on someone else.

She got busy and it wasn't until she heard a pair of heels stomping across the floor that she looked up and saw Julie, almost pouting, going back to her office. She couldn't help but smile and went back to what she was doing.

It was after lunch when she was paid a visit by Gerry who wanted to confirm that she'd distributed her important portfolios so they were looked after. She confirmed that they were and then told him that Julie seemed a little upset about something earlier.

"Don't worry about her, I'll deal with her later," Gerry told her. "If you want, you can get ready and go. You may as well."

She smiled at him. She knew he was probably right because she couldn't start anything anyway. "I'll just finish this up, set up an auto-reply on my email, and then go," she said. "Thank you."

"Do me a favour," Gerry said. "Just have fun and relax."

Lisa nodded and saluted him. "Yes Sir."

Gerry left her office and went in the direction of Julie's.

Again Lisa smiled inwardly and began to get ready to go and within half an hour she was waving at Gerry as she passed his office and she was free. She almost ran to the car and found it difficult to restrain herself as she didn't want to appear *too* excited about this.

She didn't drive straight home, instead she went to her favourite little clothing shop and bought a few new outfits as well as a couple of semi-formal dresses just in case the occasion arose that she'd go out. She wasn't ruling out meeting someone though it wasn't on her agenda. She also thought perhaps she'd go out for dinner a few times and didn't know what she'd need to do so.

On her way home, she didn't really want to, but she ended up stopping in at her parents' to say goodbye to them and let them know where it was she would be staying and that her cell number would be the best way to get in touch with her. She explained that she wasn't certain about the rest of her time off and she'd try to be in touch when she knew the rest of her plans.

She went home and just sat out on her balcony for a few minutes taking some deep breaths and trying to rid herself of work and her parents before she made herself some supper and began packing for her adventure.

It wasn't that late when she went to bed but had difficulties falling asleep and ended up reading for a lot longer than she had wanted to. She finally fell asleep and dreamed of what was to come.

CHAPTER 3

She woke the next morning excited, yet nervous about her journey. She had breakfast and finished packing, double and triple checking to make sure she had everything she would need for the duration she was gone including her laptop and her toothbrush. She rechecked the map she'd printed off the internet and when she had everything packed in the car, she went back inside, took a last look around her place, double checked that she'd set the timer for lights and locked the door behind her.

It was an hour later when Lisa turned and looked at the bare road behind her. She knew nobody would be there but she certainly felt like she was running away from something. She recounted how she'd managed to get this much time off of work. She understood they were her holidays to take, it was September and most of the staff had taken their time through the summer and she, not having anywhere to go, had waited.

She checked her directions and made the next turn, her final turn until her destination. She had found, on the internet, a large manor house built at the turn of the century that was alleged to be haunted. That wasn't what was drawing her there, it was the lake, Lake Huron, that was the draw for her.

Not long after, she turned left into a gravel driveway and followed it around trees and eventually in front of a huge manor house that stood white and majestic with the blue lake as the backdrop. She sucked in a breath at the vision and reached into the seat beside her to get her camera. She only stepped out of the car to take a shot before she got back in and finished the drive around the circle and pulled into what appeared to be parking spots, man-made over time, overgrown with weeds.

She was just getting out of the car when an older man came walking over to her. He smiled at her. "You must be Lisa, I've been waiting for you," he told her. "I saw you take a picture of the house," he added trying to start a conversation and help her feel at ease.

"Yes, the view, it was breathtaking with the house and lake..." she trailed off.

Martin was nodding at her. "I'm your host, Martin, we spoke on the phone," he said as he extended his hand.

Lisa took it cautiously and almost felt sparks at his touch. When she looked back up at his face, she felt as if she knew him from somewhere but didn't dare say that.

Martin pulled his hand away quicker than he'd wanted to. *She's going to think I don't like her,* he thought but felt he'd had no choice. It was as though electricity had passed between them and when she'd looked at him, he was drawn to her green eyes like a magnet. "Um, do you need any help carrying anything?" he asked.

Lisa took a second to process the question he'd just asked her. It was like coming out of a dream state. "Uh, yes, I have several bags," she replied swinging her hand in the direction of the car.

"Then let's get you inside and settled. Lunch is just about ready so I have to go check on it," Martin told her.

Lisa opened the rear car door and handed him some of
her bags. She grabbed her purse, the camera and the few
other items she'd had with her in the front seat for the drive
and nodded to let Martin know she was all set.

Martin turned and walked toward the house
wondering where the red-haired, green-eyed beauty came
from and how he might know her.

Lisa followed Martin looking at the back of his greying
head of hair. Her mind wandered back to the shock she'd felt
at shaking his hand and again wondered where she may
know him from. For some reason, she wanted to reach up
and run her fingers through that hair. That sent other
feelings she had wanted to keep stowed away to the surface
and she sighed. This wasn't what she was bargaining for
when she'd decided on a vacation.

"If you follow me, I'll show you straight to your room.
You can freshen up and join me for lunch if you'd like,"
Martin told her. "Free of charge of course," he added with a
smile. He realized he'd made more than enough for the two
of them knowing she'd be arriving around the lunch hour and
would probably be hungry. He also didn't realize until now
that he'd had another agenda and that was to not eat lunch
alone. In fact he'd even planned dinner with his guest in
mind.

"Thank you," Lisa replied as she took in her
surroundings as best she could with her arms full and
watching where Martin was going. He led her up a wide
staircase and then off to the left where three doors stood
closed to the hallway. He stopped outside the first one that
not only held the number '1' in brass italic but also had a
plate on the door 'Sophia's Suite'.

"You may stay in here, it's the best I have," he told her
and led her into the room where he set her bags on the floor
next to the bed. "It is now that I leave you to tend to lunch
but it will be served in a mere quarter of an hour," he said

trying desperately to sound formal yet knowing somehow he'd failed miserably.

Lisa smiled at him and tried not to laugh. "Thank you," she said again in a small voice.

Martin left the room with a nod, closing the door behind him and letting out the breath he didn't realize he'd been holding.

Lisa sucked in a deep breath and sighed. She looked around the room and saw everything was flowers. The curtains, the bedspread, even the chair coverings. It was a large room with a rocker next to a window with a window seat. A fireplace was set against the same wall and after she noticed a second window with a window seat. There was, of course, the standard dresser for her to put her things into and a well hidden closet. It wasn't until she opened the closet door to hang her jacket away that she realized it was a walk-through closet and on the other side was a beautiful, romantic bathroom complete with a Jacuzzi tub built for two and a separate shower.

She didn't have time to put the rest of her things away before lunch so she freshened up in the bathroom, changed into something a little cooler as it was warmer than she'd anticipated and found her way back downstairs. She was lost when she got to the bottom of the staircase so she looked left into the large sitting room and right into a formal dining room.

"Follow my voice," Martin called.

Lisa smiled and continued down the hall that led behind the staircase to a door through which was the kitchen. "It smells wonderful," she said as she passed through.

"It's homemade soup, hope you like it," he said as he began filling the bowls he had strategically placed at the island bar.

"I do," Lisa replied as she sat in one of the stools.

"What would you like to drink?" Martin asked and proceeded to list what was in the refrigerator, his head disappearing inside.

Lisa giggled at this before she answered and told him a glass of milk would do fine.

Once he'd poured two glasses, Martin placed the jug between them and sat down next to her.

They ate in silence for a few minutes, Lisa taking deep breaths trying to calm herself at this, the start of her vacation; and Martin, having a hard time taking his eyes off her and giving sidelong glances as often as he could.

"So what brings you here?" Martin asked.

Lisa swallowed, she had been afraid of this question coming up and knew, no matter where she was in her four weeks, she'd be asked the same thing. "I needed to get away from, well, life," she began.

"Sounds heavy," Martin replied as he stuck another spoonful of soup in his mouth.

Lisa took a sip of milk. *Here goes,* she thought. "I'm a financial advisor for one of the big banks and it's not the job, it's the pressures of the job sometimes. I don't know if that's what I'm meant to continue doing or not..."

"So you're doing some soul searching?" Martin interrupted her and instantly felt badly for doing so. He took a bite of his roll.

"Yes and no, but I feel pressure all around, family, friends, even at church right now," she went on before she took a bite of her roll after dipping it in her soup. "Everyone wants me to get married and have kids but every guy out there is macho, self-centered, egotistical..."

"Okay, okay," Martin said putting his hand up. "I get the idea."

Lisa laughed in spite of herself. "Everyone *my* age," she explained. "But it's true, they all think the world revolves around them, plus, well, like I said, I'm not sure I'm meant to continue doing what I'm doing at my job. I did some research and I was just so drawn to this place, the lake, everything."

Martin nodded. "I understand. I was drawn here too a year ago when I saw the place up for sale."

"Really?" Lisa asked.

Martin nodded again. "I was looking at retiring when I happened to see the ad for this place in a flyer that had been circulated down home for some reason and I called."

"Where did you live before?" Lisa asked, now curious about her host.

"I lived in Kitchener," he told her.

"I live in Waterloo," she replied quickly. Kitchener and Waterloo were neighbours and commonly referred to as Kitchener-Waterloo.

They looked at each other for what felt like forever before either of them spoke.

Each separately wondered what it was that had brought them here, she young, he older, and what it was they were going to discover together.

"Wow, that's amazing," Martin spoke quietly. "Listen, I..."

"It is," Lisa cut him off. "I don't know what to think right now."

Martin shook his head. "Listen, I want to show you around, make you feel at home here, please don't be afraid to ask for anything," he told her.

"Martin, I honestly don't even know what I want right now," she said. "I came here because of a legend, I came here because I needed more than anything else to get away from everything. I ran away in every sense of the word. And here I am having lunch with you and talking to you like you've been my best friend my whole life. I don't understand what's going on and I'm truly scared."

Martin smiled and reached for her hand. He took it in his and examined it for a moment as he felt the electricity exchange between them once more. It had been a long time since he'd held the hand of a woman, let alone one as beautiful as Lisa, sitting before him in all her innocent glory. "I don't know what's going on here either Lisa, but I think we need to trust a higher power to lead us in the right direction."

Lisa only looked at him. She hadn't come here for a religious lesson either though she was a strong believer in a higher power. Prayer was one of the mainstays in her life and she wasn't about to change that. But what she was being told right now was to throw caution to the wind and that she could trust this man. She smiled and she leaned over and placed a gentle kiss on his cheek. "Thank you Martin," she whispered.

Martin smiled again and released her hand. "This afternoon I'm going to show you around."

Lisa looked at him. "I am going to take a nap this afternoon too," she said.

"That sounds fine, maybe I'll join you," Martin replied and then realized how that must have sounded. "I..."

Lisa raised her fingers to his lips. "I know what you meant," she said. "At least I think I do."

Martin laughed. For some reason he wanted to do nothing more than to carry her off to her room and wrap her in his arms for the entire afternoon. He felt very protective of her and wanted to do all he could to make her stay comfortable and relaxed if nothing else.

Lisa watched as the wrinkles around his eyes appeared as he laughed. She realized the years between them but didn't care. Suddenly none of this made sense, yet all of it made sense on a subconscious level.

"Why don't you go lie down and I'll clean up the kitchen. I'll come get you when I'm finished."

Lisa nodded and reluctantly left the kitchen to do just that.

CHAPTER 4

"Help me," a voice cried from the distance, "help me please."

Lisa woke with a start and went to one of her bedroom windows that looked out over the rear of the property which led to the beach. All she could see was water. She couldn't see anyone out there and wondered what she had been dreaming about. She heard footsteps on the stairs and looked at the clock to see how long she'd slept, hoping Martin hadn't forgotten to wake her or that he was going to take her on a tour. She looked around the room and realized she hadn't unpacked yet but as she lifted her bag back onto the bed someone began knocking on her door.

"Are you okay?" Martin's voice came through.

Lisa went to the door and opened it. "I'm fine, why?" she asked.

"I heard you yell," he answered. He leaned down, his hands on his knees to catch his breath.

"I just woke up, it wasn't me, I heard it too," Lisa stammered.

"It came from up here, you said 'help me, help me please'," he said.

"I heard that too, it's what woke me," Lisa told him again. "Come in here and sit down will you," she ordered.

Martin went in and sat on the edge of the bed next to her suitcase.

"I'm just going to finish unpacking, catch your breath." Lisa smiled at him and reached into her suitcase. She suddenly became very aware of the pink satin nightgown with matching robe that was folded carefully on top and she blushed. Her eyes met Martin's and he smiled back at her.

"Oh hell," he said out loud as he reached over before she could react and pulled her by the waist over to him.

Lisa didn't know what to think of this. She didn't know what was going on and was so confused by all of it that she didn't really care either. His hands were warm through her shirt and she now stood with his legs straddling her. She looked down at him uncertain of what to do next but his hands did everything for her. They slid inside her own hands and gently tugged her downward and before she knew it, his lips had claimed hers in an extremely sensual kiss. His lips were soft and warm and his tongue gently prodded against her lips until she opened them slightly to let his tongue explore her mouth and intertwine with her own.

Martin didn't know what the hell he was doing but was very aware that Lisa was letting him. He hadn't intended on doing this and she was certainly his first guest of the many he'd had over the summer, who he'd been drawn to so very desperately. It was as if they'd known each other for a lifetime and then some. Her lips were so soft and warm and inviting. She had parted her lips so now his tongue tasted hers. His hands slid out of hers and up her arms and in a bold move he touched her breasts. He held each one in his hands and they fit there perfectly, warm and supple. His brain was no longer functioning rationally as he ran his thumb across where her nipples would be beneath her clothing.

Lisa sucked in a breath at his touch. Nobody had ever touched her breasts that way and she wanted more. She was no longer thinking rationally either and she pulled her blouse from her jeans so he could reach beneath.

Martin found this to be extremely erotic and as his hands touched her flesh for the first time he knew he had to have her. There was no turning back. He reached around her to undo the clasp of her bra and cupped her breasts. It was torture pulling his lips from hers but he had to taste. Lifting the blouse, his lips found her breast and he began suckling gently, his tongue making circles around her nipple.

Lisa sucked in another breath and didn't know how much longer she could stay standing there. Her hands circled his head and her fingers slid through the hair at the nape of his neck as she heard him suck in a breath before he switched to the other breast. She arched her back towards him. She wanted him to have all of her. She began unbuttoning the blouse and let it fall away as well as her bra. His mouth moved to her stomach and his tongue flicked her belly button.

Martin couldn't stand this for much longer and he stood quickly, rid the bed of the suitcase and eased her onto it as he undid the button and her fly and slid her pants and panties off. He kneeled between her legs and parted them before his mouth claimed her there, and she gasped again. He did his best to undress as he did this so when he knew she was ready, he could move above her and enter her. He wanted to feel her all around him. He'd been married for 30 years before his wife passed away and he'd never wanted anyone the way he wanted Lisa.

Lisa couldn't take anymore. "Oh God Martin, I need to feel you inside me, please," she begged.

Martin knew it was time and he stretched himself over her and entered her in one swift movement. She felt amazing and she moaned as he entered her. She was soft and warm and he felt like he'd gone home.

Lisa had an overwhelming sense of belonging. Like he belonged inside her and she in his arms. She almost wanted to devour him that's how wonderful he felt.

His lips claimed hers again as they began moving as one and it was a shock to both of them when their breathing changed and they both cried out at the same time, Martin lowering himself over her unable to hold himself up and they both tried desperately to catch their breath.

After a few moments of deep breathing, Martin spoke one word. "Wow!"

"It's never been like that for me before," Lisa whispered, still panting.

"Me either," Martin said between gulps for air. "But it was wonderful."

Lisa only nodded as Martin's lips claimed hers again in a very gentle kiss this time and she knew he'd claimed her as his own, despite their short time knowing each other.

Without knowing it, Lisa fell asleep after that, comforted by being in Martin's arms.

Martin watched her sleep. Her face was so innocent, so young with only a few lines around her eyes and her mouth. *What did we do?* He wondered. *What is she going to think of me?* His eyes fluttered, then closed as well and they slept that way until the sun began to set.

"Oh shit," Martin said waking rather suddenly.

"Huh? What is it?" Lisa said groggily.

"I'm sorry, I didn't mean to wake you, I didn't even know what I was doing," Martin said as he brushed a strand of hair from Lisa's face and smiled down at her. "Did you sleep well?" he asked.

Lisa nodded and yawned. What had happened beforehand came back to her and she didn't know how to feel. She didn't feel regret, she didn't feel like she'd done something wrong, she felt satisfied. For the first time in a long time she felt sated and happy.

"I think we missed dinner," Martin told her as he pointed at the window. "And I missed giving you a tour."

Lisa looked out the window beyond the foot of the bed and noticed the sun was very low in the sky and it was getting quite dark. "There's always tomorrow for a tour," she reminded him.

He nodded. "Listen, I'm going to make this up to you, do you have anything fancy to wear in there?" he asked pointing at the open suitcase now on the floor.

Lisa smiled remembering how it had found its way to the floor. She nodded. "I brought a little of everything."

"Good, put on something really nice and meet me downstairs in a half hour," Martin told her.

"Ok," Lisa replied hesitantly. She was still wrapped in his arms and wasn't sure she wanted him to go just yet.

Martin looked down at her and before he could think about it, he kissed her. Her mouth tasted and felt just as wonderful as it had earlier and he had a hard time breaking away from her but knew that they did need to eat and it was already late enough.

Lisa let him pull away from her and instantly felt cold. "See you soon," she told him.

He winked at her and gathered up his clothes before he left the room.

Lisa stayed on the bed for a moment and stared up at the ceiling. *What happened, and how did that happen?* She wondered. She was trying so hard to sort out all her feelings. Only twelve hours before she'd been running away from an old life, hoping desperately to find a reprieve from the stresses of life and put her own life and future in perspective. She wasn't even here half that time and she was already having sex with the owner of the B&B she'd chosen. But again there were no feelings of regret, only satisfaction, yet yearning, the need for him to take her back into his arms and make love to her all over again. She groaned with frustration and slid out of bed. She unpacked the rest of her things quickly and went into the bathroom where she turned the shower on and stood under the hot water wishing that Martin would appear to help her.

Martin stood under the hot spray of his own shower kicking himself in the behind. *How did I let this happen?* He asked himself over and over. *She must think I'm a complete cad. Probably figures I do this with all my single female guests.* He stepped out of the shower, dried off and started shaving. He would show her a great time tonight. Despite how awful he felt about their afternoon foray, he didn't want to lose her either. In fact he wanted her to stay indefinitely. He had ideas he hadn't had in years and that was scaring him. He went to his closet and pulled out a white shirt, his black suit and a black tie. He dressed quickly and went downstairs to the kitchen where he pulled some of the flowers he always had on hand out of their bucket and bundled them with some ribbon.

He was just getting back to the front foyer as Lisa was coming down the stairs and he almost dropped the flowers. "You look wonderful," he told her. He couldn't avoid looking at her legs, clad in black nylon, under the short black dress she was wearing. She'd let her wavy auburn hair down and it gently framed her face. She smiled at him and he melted. "I want to take you back to bed," he told her as she approached him.

"Save that for later," she replied not wanting to let on her thoughts in the shower. "Are these for me?" she asked turning her attention to the flowers.

"Yes, we'll put them in a vase and get going," he told her.

She followed him to the kitchen and watched as he cut the stems and put them in a vase.

"You can put them in your room later," he told her. "Let's go." He led her to the door and made sure she would be warm enough before he opened it for her and waited for her to walk out ahead of him. He locked up and turned to her. "Are you ready?" he asked.

Lisa nodded as he slid his hand over hers and led the way to his minivan parked next to her car. She giggled while he opened the door for her and waited for her to get in before he rounded the vehicle and got in himself. "Where are we going?" she asked.

"We're going to a restaurant in town that I enjoy visiting very much."

He held her hand on the short drive and again told her to stay put so he could open her door and help her out. His hand somehow brushed her leg and he thought he was going to lose it at that moment but he managed to compose himself and led her inside.

The restaurant was quiet as most of the regulars were seasonal and had gone home leaving the few year-round folk only. They were seated at a cozy table hidden from view near a warm fireplace and handed menus. Martin ordered a bottle of wine and the waiter left them alone.

"I have no recommendations, everything on the menu is wonderful," Martin said and winked at her.

Lisa tried to turn her attention to the menu but all she could focus on was Martin's leg touching hers under the table. She could hear music coming from somewhere and looked over her menu to the corner where couples kept disappearing.

"We're going over there later," Martin said as he watched her.

Lisa turned her attention back to her menu and decided on something simple like the Chicken Caesar Platter and closed her menu. She didn't feel very hungry, certainly not for food, and smiled nervously at Martin.

"Everything okay?" he asked as he too set aside his menu.

Lisa nodded. "I'm fine, I think I'm just a little overwhelmed from the days' events."

Martin nodded, "I can understand that," he replied. "This isn't something I do everyday."

"So what do you do everyday?" Lisa asked without thinking.

"I run the B and B. I clean it up, I answer the phone, I cook, I take care of all of the gardening, I buy the groceries, I do the laundry and once breakfast is served and my arrivals are accounted for, I get to do a few of the things I want but I don't get a lot of spare time until this time of year. I certainly do *not* make it a habit of chasing my young female guests."

Lisa laughed. "So I'm the first," she stated, though partially posing it as a question.

"Yes, you *are* the first and perhaps maybe the last," he told her hinting at something far grander than even Lisa could imagine. *What am I thinking?* He asked himself. *She's practically half my age*, he pointed out.

Lisa only looked at him, entirely uncertain of what he meant by that last comment. If it was what she thought it was, then she was taking it very well. She hadn't thought of that but it wasn't something that she would deny either.

The waiter returned, breaking the silence that had come between them and after Martin tried the wine and okayed it, the waiter filled both glasses and took their orders.

Martin picked up his glass and motioned for her to do the same. "I'd like to make a toast to a new friendship," he said.

Lisa pressed her glass against his and then took a sip. She set the glass on the table in front of her and looked

Martin in the eye. "Where exactly do you see this going?" she asked.

Martin could only shrug his shoulders. "I don't know," he told her. "It wasn't something I planned, as I said, so I'm lost at sea."

Lisa nodded. This was all new territory for her as well and where it would lead she wasn't sure and she wasn't sure she wanted to know at this point.

When they finished eating, they waited for dessert and had more wine to drink before Martin took her hand and led her behind the wall where all the people kept disappearing.

Lisa was shocked to see a band set up and more people dancing than she thought was in the restaurant.

Martin took her into his arms and acknowledged how very right it felt to him. His arm circled her waist perfectly and her hand fit easily into his.

Lisa smiled, aware herself how right it felt to her too. His words from earlier rang in her ears and she wondered if he was going to propose. It was certainly the perfect environment, all dressed up, dinner, dancing. Why not a proposal? Then she realized this was only the first evening of her visit though it felt like she'd not only been away for years but it also felt that she'd known Martin that long too.

Martin didn't want the night to end. He wanted to keep her right here in his arms for the rest of the night and for all eternity if he could. He was still amazed at how relaxed they were with each other and still couldn't figure out exactly what was going on. He'd had the urge to propose but knew that might just be the one thing that would scare her away so he chose to not go that far... just yet. He spun her around the floor with the ease of years of experience and watched her as she smiled at him, with all the trust in the world.

He took her back to the house that night and instead of leading her to her room, he led her the other way to his own where he slowly and seductively undressed her, stopping to kiss her mouth, her neck, her collarbone and eventually her breasts before he again slid his tongue inside her. He made love to her with every ounce of his being and when they climaxed together, he gathered her into his arms and they whispered quietly in the dark until they fell asleep both fully aware of what was going on, but both as confused as the other as to how all of it had happened so quickly and what other forces were bringing them together on this journey.

CHAPTER 5

Lisa woke the next more with a bit of stiffness in her neck as she'd spent the night with her head on Martin's shoulder. She looked around the room and admired how this room had been decorated similar to the other and never would have thought it to be a man's room. She spotted the sun streaming from behind a doorway and assumed that's what she was looking for and carefully slid from Martin's arms and walked towards it. She smiled when she saw it was the bathroom and she closed the door quietly and went about freshening herself up a bit. She eyed the shower and thought how wonderful that would feel but thought she would wait. She still didn't know what Martin would and wouldn't approve of and using his shower might be overdoing it.

After she'd splashed some cold water on her face and slurped up some water out of her hands so she could rinse her mouth, she slowly opened the door and began to tiptoe back to the bed when Martin opened his eyes.

"Busted," he said with a grin on his face.

Lisa smiled at him. She did not feel embarrassed by the fact she was naked. "Next time I'm going to just go ahead and take a shower," she told him.

"You could have, I wouldn't have stopped you. I probably would have joined you," he told her.

"I figured you would have joined me, but I didn't know if you'd appreciate me using your shower," she told him.

"Why wouldn't I?" he asked.

"Because it's *your* personal space," she replied quietly.

Martin moved closer to the edge of the bed and reached up to her waist and pulled her closer. His tongue slid up her thigh before he slid it inside her and listened while she moaned. He stopped only for a moment so he could finish what he was saying. "If we can be this intimate darling, my shower is your shower."

Lisa kneeled on the bed and Martin pulled her closer to him so he could continue what he was doing and make her crazy for him.

It was another hour before they climbed out of bed and since there were no other guests, they wore their robes to the kitchen and ate breakfast, teasing each other, reaching to touch each other and when they had finished, Martin led Lisa back upstairs to his bedroom and went in the shower with her where he made love to her again. He felt like a schoolboy even though he had just celebrated his 57th birthday.

After they dressed, Martin led her down to the beach where he took her hand and they walked quietly along the water's edge. It was still really warm so the lake water had yet to cool and every now and again Lisa would see a stone or a shell she wanted and would let go of his hand to pick it up. She felt cold and alone when she did and quickly returned her hand to his.

They stopped every so often and kissed and returned to walking. Lisa thought she could do this forever and realized that she only had four weeks to not only make up her mind but she'd already booked herself in at another B&B

before she'd left. She got very quiet and started thinking seriously about what it was she wanted. She didn't have much time.

"What are you thinking?" Martin asked pulling her to him and tilting her chin up to look at her face.

"I'm thinking I have a booking at another B&B for two days from now," she told him.

Martin's face drew serious. "Please stay," he said quietly. "I don't know what's happening here but I really want to find out." He paused for what felt like forever. "And, well, I think..." he bit his lip.

Lisa knew what was coming and she felt butterflies in her stomach. Something told her what he was going to say but she couldn't help asking anyway, "what?" she asked just as quietly.

"I love you," he said. "I have loved you since I shook your hand in the driveway and felt the electricity shoot up my arm," he told her.

Lisa smiled. "I felt the same thing. I love you too and I don't want to go which is what I was thinking about. I want to call and cancel. I just can't go on right now. I have enough future decisions to make based on this moment in time," she said.

Martin looked at her for a moment before he realized she had to return to work, that she was just on vacation, a long vacation but still a vacation and he nodded. "We have a branch in town you know," he said referring to the bank she worked for.

Lisa's eyes grew wide for a moment and she reached up and pulled his head down to give him a kiss.

Martin turned around and they walked slowly back to the house. He was determined to make her happy, he just didn't know exactly how yet. He led her straight to the bedroom where he made love to her again and held her tightly in his arms. He didn't want to let her go.

"I have to get into town," Martin said after he'd held her for a while as she slept.

Lisa looked at him questioningly.

"I need to get some groceries or we can't eat," he told her. "Besides, it will give you a chance to use the phone and cancel your next stop," he added.

Lisa nodded in agreement. She felt the need to be alone too for a little while so they dressed and Martin kissed her goodbye.

Martin went to the van and smiled. It had been a while since he'd had someone to kiss goodbye at the door or greet him when he returned for that matter. His heart was telling him what to do but he wasn't sure if he could rationalize it, or go through with it. There was certainly more than one thing he had to do when he got to town. He gave a wave before he left the driveway.

After Martin left, Lisa went to her room and found the papers she'd scribbled the information on and made the call to cancel her next stop. They were actually quite relieved to hear from her as they'd received an urgent call about a family member who'd had a heart attack and they knew that they had no way of connecting with her.

Lisa set the phone down in the cradle. She hadn't made any plans beyond that next stop and she was confused. She put her papers away, went to the kitchen where she made herself a cup of tea but instead of putting it into a tea cup, she put it into one of the many travel mugs she found in the cupboard and went down to the beach for another walk. She walked quietly along listening to the waves hitting the shore. She stopped and looked out over the water, blue, clear, and shimmering with the reflection of the sun. She wondered what had just happened. The thought had crossed her mind when she got off the phone but it took until now for it to finally surface in her mind. She took in the scenery

again—the water, the sun, the clouds in the sky, all of it God's
creation and how little she looked to him sometimes. She
was active at church, which was part of what had brought her
here, but she didn't pray a lot outside of church and she
didn't have 'talks' with God that some people talked about.
Yet she believed in a higher power with all of her being and
she knew that there were ways for Him to intervene and she
suddenly felt like this was one of them. She sipped her tea
and let the waves wash over her feet. She was still surprised
by how warm the water was since it was September.

She walked along and collected a few more stones as
well as some shells. She didn't know yet what she would do
with them but she was forming an idea for that in her mind
as well.

It was as she was walking back up the beach that she
realized how far she'd walked and how much thinking she
must have done. When she tried to take a sip of tea, she
realized the cup was empty and she smiled as the breeze from
the lake pushed her hair away from her face. She wanted to
see a sunset out here yet and planned on doing so that
evening just in case every other evening she was here was a
rainy one. She reached the bottom of the steps and took one
last look over the lake before turning to go back up to the
house.

She rinsed her cup out and left it on the rack to dry
and walked upstairs feeling guilty for leaving a trail of sand
behind her from her feet.

She ran some water into the tub and sat on the edge
swishing her feet back and forth watching as the sand came
off.

A strong pair of arms wrapped themselves around her
and a pair of warm lips kissed her neck. "I missed you,"
Martin whispered in her ear before he nibbled at her earlobe.

Lisa smiled. "I missed you too," she replied as she
tilted her head back to allow access to her throat.

"What are you doing?" he asked. His hands cupped her breasts through her t-shirt.

"I went for a walk on the beach and my feet got all sandy, I'm rinsing them off," she told him. "I'm sorry about the mess I made."

"I don't care about the mess," he murmured. He helped her turn around and dried her feet for her before he led her to the bed and began undressing her. "I really did miss you."

They made love, Martin taking extra care and it was when they both climaxed that they blurted out "I love you," to one another.

After they had caught their breath, Lisa made sure she told Martin she wanted to see the sunset that night.

Martin didn't have a problem with that at all. That had been his goal the previous night so he wouldn't allow himself to fall asleep and miss it again. "I'd love to see that with you," he told her. "I am going to go start supper now though."

Lisa nodded. "I'm going to sit in the kitchen with you and we're going to get to know each other a little better than we do. Oh, and I got in touch with Jim at the next B&B and they were actually glad to hear from me. *They* needed to cancel my reservation."

Martin looked at her with as much surprise on his face as Lisa had had on hers when she'd headed to the beach.

She followed him to the kitchen and ended up helping him put dinner together and then they retreated to the sitting room where they chatted until dinner was ready.

After dinner, they tidied up quickly as it was starting to get a little darker outside and Lisa ran upstairs to get her camera.

Martin was waiting by the back door for her and they crossed the yard and stood at the top of the stairs watching as the sun slowly sank in the sky before them coming closer and closer to the water's edge.

When it reached the max and the sky turned different shades of red and pink, Lisa stood snapping pictures and Martin sank down onto one knee.

"Lisa," Martin said.

Lisa turned her attention to him and was surprised he was on the ground.

"I know we don't know each other very well at all, but something neither of us can explain has happened in the last two days. I fell in love with you as soon as you got out of your car yesterday and even though this sounds absurd, I also feel like I have no other choice, will you marry me Lisa?"

Lisa looked at him and she looked at the sunset. It was the perfect end to a perfect day, though confusing, and she felt the breeze through her hair and she felt Martin's hand on hers. She could also feel his eyes watching her face, waiting so patiently for her to give him her answer. She had been drawn here, she had felt a deep need to be here. Other than work and family, what other reasons were there to not accept his proposal? She had no reasons. No *valid* reasons whatsoever that she could think of that would not allow her to say 'yes'. She looked once again at the setting sun, suspended over the lake as if it too was waiting to hear her answer. It was as if the time-space continuum had all but stopped just to wait for her answer. She looked back down at Martin and her eyes met his and she began to nod.

"Yes, Martin, I will marry you. Oh my God," she replied.

Martin let out a huge sigh as if he'd been holding his breath forever.

Lisa looked out over the lake and noticed the sun was once again descending into the water. She looked back at Martin who was fumbling with the ring in the box and she felt her hands trembling.

"Got it," he said and he allowed the box to drop to the ground as he lifted her left hand in his and slid the ring onto her ring finger.

Lisa admired the gorgeous cut diamond and smiled. "Thank you," she said quietly.

Martin led her back to the house after he'd picked up the box and the sun had disappeared into the lake.

Without a word, they locked up and turned out all the lights before they climbed the stairs and Lisa followed Martin once again to his bedroom where he made love to her over and over until they were both completely exhausted and they fell asleep.

CHAPTER 6

When Lisa woke the next morning she was certain she'd been dreaming. She moved a little in bed and realized she was alone. Her mind recalled Martin's proposal on the beach at sunset and she was positive she'd been dreaming. She never thought to even look at her left hand and then she heard the door opening and rolled over to see Martin carrying a tray with breakfast.

"What time is it?" Lisa asked.

"It's 9:00 my dear," Martin replied. "Did you sleep well?"

Lisa thought about that for a second and nodded. "I think I was dreaming," she said first.

"Well I thought I'd bring you some coffee," he said and held a mug out for her.

Lisa reached for it and saw the ring on her finger. She sucked in a breath.

"Is something wrong?" Martin asked still holding the cup.

"Um, I guess I wasn't dreaming," she replied. She realized he was still holding her coffee and finally took it from him.

Martin smiled at her. "We had a busy day yesterday," he said.

"Yeah, I guess we did," she agreed and took a sip of the coffee. "This is really good," she told him and set the cup back down on the tray.

"Well, help yourself to breakfast; I thought breakfast in bed would be a nice touch," Martin said waving a hand over the tray.

Lisa smiled and helped herself to some of the pancakes he'd made.

"I guess we have a few details to work out," Martin said quietly.

Lisa sucked in a breath. She wasn't quite prepared for all of this. "Look, I know we have things to talk about and I certainly have a few things to work out but can we just put it on hold for at least a day or two? I'm just really overwhelmed right now," she told him.

Martin held up his hands. "I'm not pressing." The reason she was here had come back to him as soon as she'd said how she felt and he felt like a heel. He should never have expected her to just jump into this all at once. She was still trying to work through everything else. "Listen, I don't know if it would help or not, or even exactly what I'm trying to say," he paused to laugh. "But I was wondering if there was anything I can do to help you work through some of your issues from home? I can be a great listener when given the chance," he offered.

Lisa nodded. She knew she really had to work through those things. "One thing at a time."

Martin nodded, "what's worse?" he asked.

Lisa shrugged her shoulders. "I'm not sure. My parents are just being really pushy and expecting me to get married," she paused for a moment to smile and look at her left hand and raised her eyebrows at Martin who laughed. "And have babies," she went on.

It was Martin's turn to frown. He wasn't sure he'd be able to help her with the latter, something they would still need to discuss.

"What's wrong?" Lisa asked.

"We'll talk about it when we start discussing 'us'," he replied.

"My sister has already been married, has a baby and has number two on the way," she explained. "And she's two years younger than I am."

Martin nodded. "So what you're saying is you really needed to run away and hide for a while?"

Lisa looked at him her eyes met his. "Yes, well, no. I need to just be able to figure out what *I* want. What's right for *me*. Not what everyone else wants from me or expects of me."

Martin now understood. "So I solved one of your problems last night by proposing?" he asked.

Lisa laughed. "I don't think it's *quite* that easy but I think you're close."

"Let's have a shower," Martin suggested. "We've worked part way through one of your problems, perhaps a walk on the beach might get you talking about what's going on at work."

Lisa nodded, it sounded like a wonderful idea, but she did want to get into town during the daytime and do some shopping so she shared this with him carefully.

Martin held up a hand. "Say no more, I have no problem with that," he replied. He again felt bad because he was pressing himself on her and he should have realized right from the start that she would want to go off and be a tourist at some point. He wondered what would have happened if she'd arrived in the middle of the summer when he'd had the rooms full of guests constantly and was checking people in and out all day long. He realized he'd pressed again and he looked at her. "I'm sorry," he said. "Feel free to do whatever you like. When you get back, I will again propose a walk on the beach again and perhaps another sunset."

Lisa looked at him and smiled. This was so different for her. She'd never before had a boyfriend, in this case fiancé, who respected her wants and needs. "Let's shower."

They both slid in under the hot water and Martin pulled her to him. His fingers slid across her wet skin and over her rounded buttock. Sliding his hand over her hip, he pulled his hips away from her far enough to let his hand slide between them and he slid his fingers inside her as deep as possible.

"Oh God," Lisa moaned.

Martin's lips covered hers and he felt her hips moving in motion with his fingers. It was extremely erotic to him and he continued to press his fingers inside her. He felt her climax and as she did so, he pressed her up against the wall and slid himself inside her feeling her muscles still contracting around him as she gasped.

Lisa wanted to call out, yet her throat was constricted. She made a few sounds but nothing coherent.

Martin took hold of her hips and his tongue reached into her mouth. She felt absolutely wonderful and he didn't want to let her go. Yet he was reaching the point of his own climax and he knew he couldn't stop it. As Lisa tilted her hips forward, he reached it and called out her name.

Lisa smiled and after they'd recovered, they finished showering and Lisa walked down the hall, wrapped in nothing more than her towel, to her room to dress.

Martin appeared only a few minutes later, after Lisa had had the chance to pull on some panties and her bra, and sucked in a breath at the sight of her. "This is ridiculous you know," he said.

"What is?" she asked.

"You dressing in here. Let's make room for your things in my room, well, our room," Martin said. "In fact if you want to leave your things out, I'll move them for you while you're gone," he added.

Lisa smiled at him. She couldn't even answer before he had crossed the room and slid her out of her bra and panties and carried her to the bed. "What are you doing?" she asked.

"I'm making love to you again, because I love you," he told her as he sank down between her legs and used his tongue to pleasure her.

"Oh God Martin, oh, deeper please," Lisa begged.

He honoured her request and thrust back and forth repeatedly.

"I want you inside me, please," Lisa cried out when she climaxed.

Martin rose above her and smiled down at her. He slid his hands under her hips and pulled her toward him sliding her right onto him. He continued to thrust as he watched her face and felt her around him. His thumb pressed against her and she cried out again and again.

Finally he shifted above her and re-entered her, his mouth claiming hers and began the ritual that would now bring him to his own climax.

Martin groaned as he got out of bed. He desperately needed to get things done around the house. He was going to need to get the grass mowed at some point before the weather started to change and there were already leaves that needed raking. Ordering firewood was another of the little chores he needed to do and he pondered how much he would need.

Lisa sat up on the other side of the bed. She certainly didn't feel like going into town now, perhaps rolling up into a ball and going to sleep would be a better option. But she also didn't want to deprive herself of being a tourist and then wondered if Martin could show her around a bit.

"I'd love to," Martin said. He set aside everything he wanted to do because he wanted to spend time with her more than do everyday chores. He thought perhaps she'd lie down later on and then he could get those things done.

They dressed and he again led her to the van and held the door for her to get in.

Lisa wondered about all of his attention she was getting and wondered if, at some point, he gets more visitors up here. She thought it odd, knowing the place was advertised as haunted, that there weren't more people desperate to see the place. That reminded her that she hadn't *felt* anything since she'd been there and wondered if perhaps it wasn't true.

"What are you thinking?" Martin asked on the drive.

"I read the house was haunted," she began.

"Oh, that rumour. Well, I've definitely not experienced much at all while I've been here."

"Have you experienced anything at all?" she asked.

"Maybe some moans and groans and some floorboards now and again but that could have been the shifting of the house or the wind for that matter," he told her.

"Well maybe it was haunted because of the people who owned it before and the ghosts like you," she speculated.

Martin shrugged his shoulders. "I don't concern myself much with the paranormal world, I'll accept it's there, don't get me wrong, but that's about the extent of it," he said.

"I kind of like that philosophy, I believe it's there too but sometimes I want to learn more about it," she said.

"That's great, learning is always going on and if you have a choice, then so be it," he replied and reached over to pat her knee.

The rest of the trip was quiet by comparison and Lisa wondered what she would find when she started her shopping.

"Listen, I'm going to drop you off here and you can start your shopping. I just need to get a few things at the hardware store and you probably won't want to go there with me."

Lisa nodded in agreement and gave him a kiss before she got out of the car.

CHAPTER 7

Once back at the house, Martin did what he needed to get done which included checking messages. One was an inquiry on rates for around Christmas time and he wasn't sure what to tell them when he called back so he waited and decided to tell Lisa, who had gone to her room to unpack what she'd purchased, that he was going to be around outside as he had several things that needed to be done.

Lisa protested and insisted that he help her move her things to his room so she could get settled there while he was outside.

Martin agreed and gladly helped her carry the things down the hall before he went back downstairs and outside.

Lisa began putting her things where she'd been told she could before she unpacked the things she had purchased during her trip into town. One of the things she had found was an old book she hoped Martin would like. She re-bagged it and slid it under her sweaters in the drawer.

She picked up one of the books she'd brought to read and settled herself on one of the window seats in Martin's room. She opened the book but ended up unable to read it as thoughts began to run through her mind so fast she almost jumped off and ran for paper and pen. She suddenly realized that she needed to work through her thoughts about returning to work because she would need to let Gerry know very soon what was going on. She was nervous about telling him that she'd become engaged as he was almost like a father to her. She also knew that as part of all that, and probably first and foremost, she needed to determine whether she really wanted to move here. Her bank had a branch in town, as she'd seen it with her own eyes today, and thought it might be possible to try and get a spot in there if that was at all possible. She wasn't sure exactly what she wanted and she suddenly wished she had more time.

"What do you look so serious about?" Martin asked when he came in for a drink of water.

Lisa had run all the way to the kitchen for paper and was madly scribbling away at the kitchen table. She wrote one more thing before she set the pen down carefully. "I wanted to read, but all these thoughts kept flooding my mind and I didn't know what else to do but to write them down," she told him. "I have a lot to think about," she said quietly as tears filled her eyes.

Martin, forgetting the drink of water, went over to her and took her into his arms. "It's because of me isn't it?" he asked.

She nodded, then shook her head. "I agreed to marry you and everything tells me that's the right thing to do, but there are other factors that I wasn't thinking of when I said 'yes' and now I have to work that out."

"Listen, don't worry about me. Whatever you decide will be fine with me. Despite loving it here, I *will* move back to the city if I need to. I will go where ever I have to just to be with you. I *love* you and nothing is going to change that no matter where we are."

The tears poured down her cheeks and Lisa couldn't believe her luck. How had she managed to find the greatest guy on the planet and what was he doing hiding out next to the lake?

Martin hugged her tighter as the tears streamed down her face. He dug in his pocket and found a tissue and handed it to her. He knew it wasn't all because of him and what he'd just said but the release of all her frustrations about everything. He held her and rocked her gently until she quieted then he gently lifted her out of the chair and carried her upstairs to the bedroom. He set her on the bed and walked into the bathroom, closing the door behind him. He turned the water on to fill the tub and added some bubble bath.

Returning to the bedroom he found Lisa the way he'd left her and he slowly and painstakingly undressed her. It was nearly impossible for him to keep his hands from wandering. He covered her with a blanket so he could check on the tub and when he was satisfied with it, he went and picked her up, after removing his own shirt, and carried her into the bathroom. He very carefully lowered her into the tub and listened to her sigh.

"You have to join me," she murmured.

"I will, very soon. I want you to have a few minutes to relax first." With that he left the room and returned to the bedroom where he paced back and forth for a few minutes, desperate to touch her, to be with her, but also wanting her to know that she would always have the space she needed. He also realized he had some thinking of his own to do, mainly whether or not he *really* wanted to leave this place despite what he'd told Lisa. Yet his heart told him the real answer which was exactly what he'd already told her. He couldn't wait a second longer and went back into the bathroom where he finished undressing and slid into the tub behind her so she could rest her head on his chest. "Hey sweetheart," he whispered in her ear.

She smiled and whispered a 'hey' back.

Martin kissed her neck and nibbled at her ear. "Feeling a little better?"

Lisa only nodded. She *was* feeling a little better but felt like she had a mountain to climb. Eventually she told him this.

"I'll be with you every step of the way and I'll understand whatever decision you make."

Lisa smiled up at him and rested her head back again and closed her eyes.

Martin just held her for a few minutes and closed his own eyes. Soon his hands were cupping her breasts.

"Make love to me," Lisa murmured.

Martin helped her out of the tub and dried her off. He took her to bed where he held her, caressed her and eventually made love to her slowly and gently.

After, he held her tight and whispered in her ear telling her he loved her and wanted to be with her and couldn't wait to marry her.

Lisa smiled, then frowned.

"What's that look for?" he asked.

"Just something else I have to work on," she told him.

Martin frowned too. "I don't want you to think of our wedding as a chore," he said more sternly than he'd planned.

"No, Martin, I didn't mean it that way," she said quickly. "But it is one more thing that I will eventually have to do."

"I'm going to make us some supper. You stay here and just rest," Martin told her.

Lisa didn't realize it was that close to supper time and realized that she really was hungry. She was also very sleepy and she just nodded at Martin and watched as he got out of bed and got dressed.

He kissed her before he left the room and felt a tugging at his heart. He was extremely worried about her and all that she had to go through.

Lisa felt her eyelids get heavier and she closed them. She had a few thoughts go through her mind but eventually fell asleep.

"Do you Lisa take Martin to be your husband, to have and to hold, love and cherish as long as you both shall live?" Lisa looked up at the minister and smiled before she said "I do."

Then she seemed to be a bystander, rather than a participant and saw herself standing there, dressed all in white, carrying a bouquet of all pink flowers, Martin standing in a tuxedo with an ascot and when she looked around, they were outside in the yard under a blue, almost indigo sky, the sun just starting to set over the lake.

"What are you smiling about?" Martin asked, whispering in her ear.

Lisa came to and was startled. She smiled when she saw Martin. "Our wedding," she said. "I was dreaming about it, kind of."

Martin asked about it and she filled him in as she dressed and he led her downstairs to the kitchen where he'd made them supper.

"I didn't realize I had even fallen asleep," Lisa said.

"I was hoping you had," he told her as he filled to glasses with wine.

After supper he led her to the den where he had built a fire and they cuddled with one another and shared with each other their family and past.

The fire was down to mere ashes when Martin stood up, helped her off the floor and led her upstairs where he tucked her into bed and a few moments later joined her. He made love to her before he pulled her into his arms and they fell asleep.

CHAPTER 8

During the night, Lisa was restless. She got up around four and went and sat downstairs by the fireplace that Martin had carefully put out before he'd taken her to bed. She looked around the dark room, just making out the shadows of the furniture and realized she hadn't spent a lot of time doing other things in the house. She realized just how large this room was and got up to go and look in the front living room. It too was huge and she began picturing the wedding reception here. Perhaps even the wedding but she remembered her dream and the wedding out in the yard and thought she might like to do that.

She went to the desk where Martin worked from when customers checked in and found a pad of paper and a pen and began to write:

Wedding in the garden

Reception in the house—perhaps a tent outside as well--? People

Go online tomorrow and check email at work as well as job postings at Goderich branch, consider emailing Gerry with news and thoughts

Maybe I want to 'retire', help Martin run this place and write a book???

She stopped at this last note for a moment and realized that perhaps that's what she wanted to do.

Call mom and Jennie and see what they have to say about my news—mom will have a cow!

She couldn't think of anything more to write so she folded up the paper and slid it into the pocket of her robe. She was beginning to feel sleepy again but wasn't sure she'd actually go to sleep right away so she went into the kitchen where she found the leftover wine from dinner and poured herself a glass. She returned to the cozy chair by the fireplace and sipped at the rich red liquid.

She was almost finished and getting quite sleep, yet a little frisky as well, when Martin startled her.

"What are you doing down here?" he asked.

She gasped and turned around.

"I'm sorry, I didn't mean to startle you, I just missed you when I woke up," he told her.

"I couldn't sleep so I came down here. I didn't want to wake you."

"So you're having a glass of wine hoping it will help you go back to sleep?" he asked.

She nodded, then realized he probably couldn't see her through the darkness. "Something like that," she replied and tipped the glass back to finish it. "I know something else that might help me go to sleep," she said as she stood but stumbled.

Martin chuckled. "Little too much to drink?" he teased.

"No, not too much to drink," she replied. "Well, maybe."

"Come on you lush, let's get you back to bed," Martin said as he went to her and slid her hand into his own. He sucked in a breath. It felt as though her hand belonged there.

He wanted to give everything to this young woman who had swept into his life three days ago. He still couldn't believe how it had happened and he also couldn't believe he had proposed and she'd said yes. Sure, he heard about these things happening but he certainly didn't think it would ever happen to him. He led her up the stairs and into the bedroom.

Lisa smiled at him and leaned close. She untied the robe and took one of his hands in hers and pressed his palm to her breast. She sucked in a breath at the touch and heat of his hand on her breast and she reached down and began stroking him.

Martin sucked in a breath. "So the wine *didn't* make you sleepy," he chuckled before his mouth claimed hers.

Soon, they were on the bed making love, Martin's hands trying to touch her everywhere at once, his mouth kissing her all over and then entering her like he'd never made love before in his life, holding himself there to just feel her warmth all around him. The closest two people could ever be, cherishing the moment.

Soon he could no longer resist the urges and within a few moments they had climaxed together, Martin falling on top of Lisa, both of them panting. He only rolled away far enough to not crush her for the rest of the night but was sure to put his arms around her.

They fell asleep after that and Lisa didn't have to worry about getting up again.

CHAPTER 9

Martin woke to the telephone ringing. He lifted his head but couldn't quite see what time it was. His arm was trapped under Lisa and he had to slowly slide it out. After their little rendezvous in the middle of the night, he wanted to let her sleep. She stirred only a little when he had only his hand to go and he pushed up on one elbow and saw it was almost ten. He almost jumped out of bed but it was too late, the call would have already gone to the voicemail. He didn't care at this point but then thought perhaps he better care because it *was* his life's investment. *Guess I have some serious thinking to do too,* he thought. Up until now it didn't really matter to him. He hadn't had too many plans to go away but now he started to think of all the places he would love to take Lisa, all the things he'd love to show her. Perhaps a romantic trip to Europe, a cruise somewhere or more than one place, suddenly he was making plans for them and he didn't know what to do either. He also had something else nagging at the back of his mind but he brushed that off. He grabbed his robe and left the room strolling slowly through the house, looking at it from ceiling to floor.

When he reached the kitchen, he made coffee and some breakfast, in as routine a fashion as if it was engrained in him already and he shook his head as he did this. Maybe he should only be open certain seasons just like some of the others, he wrote that down on a pad next to the phone, then he picked up the phone and dialed in for his messages. He sighed with relief when he heard it was the people who had called the previous day telling him he didn't have to call them back, they had chosen to take a cruise instead. Before he logged out, he pressed all the appropriate buttons that would lead him to his message and he before he realized what he was doing, he had changed his message to say he was now closed until the spring. He felt relief spread through him when he hung up though and he prepared a tray of coffee and food and carried it upstairs.

"Morning beautiful," he whispered in Lisa's ear and kissed her neck. Her auburn hair lay across the pillow shining from the streaks of sunlight that streamed through a crack in the blinds.

Lisa only murmured something that resembled a good morning and rolled over to look at Martin. "You alright?" she asked.

"I'm okay," he replied.

"You sure?" she pressed. She knew something was up but she wasn't sure if it was good or bad.

"I'm just working on something myself at the moment," he told her. "Don't worry about it yet, I *will* discuss it with you, but like you I have a few things to work out."

Lisa smiled. "I smell coffee," she said.

"You do," he said. He picked up the tray and showed it to her before he set it back down again. He was going to prop the pillows up behind her but she was quicker than he was and sat on the edge of the bed and slid into her own robe as Martin looked on.

He moaned deep in his throat at the sight of her. He thought he would never get used to looking at her beautiful body. That he would always be in awe over her creamy skin, perfect figure and gorgeous breasts.

They sat at the small table in front of the back window and looked out over the lake.

"It's a good day," Lisa said.

Martin nodded. I think we should take a drive today. I can find you lots more shopping," he told her. "If you don't mind sitting in the car that is," he added quickly.

A smile spread across Lisa's face. "I'd love to," she replied as she caught a glimpse of the ring that was on her finger. "Where to?" she asked.

"I'm suggesting a trip to Bayfield," he told her. "If you excuse me I'll make a quick call or two, then we'll get ready to go."

Lisa nodded and took another sip of her coffee as Martin left the room. He was being kind of secretive but she didn't figure it was going to be dangerous in any way. When she finished her coffee, she set down her mug and went to the bathroom where she turned on the water and slid under the shower. She began washing her hair when a strong pair of arms wrapped around her from behind. "Morning," she replied.

"It's all set, we'll pack up and get on the road a little later on. I called on a peer of mine who agreed to let us stay over tonight and I've made reservations for dinner so make sure you pack something really nice," he told her.

"Sounds wonderful," Lisa said as she rinsed her hair. As she leaned forward to get her conditioner, Martin slid a hand between her legs and began caressing her. Lisa gasped and reached for the bar on the tub surround.

She climaxed and sank onto the tub edge to catch her breath for a few moments. When she had, she let Martin wash her with her sponge before she stepped out. She dried off and wrapped the towel around her still very much aware of what Martin had done and that her legs still felt shaky. She took one of her smaller travel bags out and began packing it. She was just about finished when Martin came out of the bathroom, naked and she couldn't help but feel very aroused. She gave a tug on the towel and let it pool at her feet.

Martin took a few swift steps forward and pulled her into his arms pushing her towards the bed. He didn't even caress her, just pressed himself inside.

After, Lisa dressed while he went about packing his things and Martin was glad he had changed the message on the voicemail giving him the freedom to be able to do this.

About half an hour later, Martin pulled up in front of the Lakefront Bed & Breakfast and the two got out of the car. Martin carried the bags and led Lisa inside. He chatted easily with the owner, Maria, who continued chatting as she led them to their rooms and told them she'd be serving tea at about 3:30 that afternoon and they were welcome to join her, she'd love to catch up with one of her 'neighbours' and find out about the beautiful woman accompanying him.

They unpacked and when Lisa sat on the bed to see what it was like, Martin attacked her. He made love to her like he'd never touched her before and she did the same.

Once they had recovered, they dressed slowly and Lisa used the bathroom to freshen up her make-up and pull her hair up as it was another gorgeous day outside, far warmer than it should be for that time of year.

Martin called to her asking if she was ready and she replied by opening the bathroom door and nodding.

Martin locked the door to their room and led her down the stairs and, with a wave to Maria, out the door. They didn't have to drive anywhere as they were right downtown and there were shops to either side of them as they looked up and down the street. Lisa was delighted as they headed out.

"You don't have to shop everywhere this afternoon, there's always tomorrow morning," he reminded her.

For a while, they each went their own way and Lisa found that she loved many of the shops she visited.

"Hey, did you want to sit down with Maria for tea?" Martin asked when he finally found her after poking his head inside several of the stores.

Lisa nodded, thanked the woman she'd just dealt with and left with a wave behind her.

They had a wonderful chat with Maria who was delighted to hear that Martin was getting married. She thought Lisa was absolutely delightful and offered her small catering service for their wedding. Lisa wrote down the information and mentally added it to the secret list that remained behind in the pocket of her bathrobe.

They returned to their suite where they showered and again made love like two teenagers and after Martin had dressed in his suit, Lisa kicked him out so she could dress for the formal evening out to dinner at The Little Inn.

Martin was standing at the bottom of the stairs talking to Maria who was telling him how sharp he looked and trying to straighten his tie when Lisa started down the stairs. She had dressed in a navy blue sleeveless dress made of velvet that hung just to her knees. She'd found it that afternoon at the last shop she'd been in and was grateful the woman had already bagged it for her before Martin had arrived.

Martin whistled at her. He was always surprised by her and she'd put her hair into spirals and it looked absolutely seductive.

When Lisa reached the bottom of the stairs and Maria and Martin had finished gaping over her choice of wardrobe she leaned into Martin and kissed his cheek.

"You only have one agenda don't you?" he teased, whispering in her ear.

She nodded. "To seduce you," she replied at an equal volume.

He grinned at her and turned to Maria who reached behind her counter and pulled out a plastic container. From inside, he pulled a corsage with small red rosettes and white baby's breath.

Lisa gasped in awe as she saw it and held her arm out for him to slide it on.

Maria had to have a picture of them before they left and they were grateful it was only a few minutes walk away as he feared they would have been late with all the attention Maria was doting on them.

Martin held out an arm for Lisa and led her out the door after she took it and a few minutes and he held the door for her at the restaurant. He gave his name and they were led to a quiet table in a corner.

"We even get some privacy," Lisa said after Martin had ordered wine and they'd been left alone.

"That's good, I can grope you without people seeing," he teased.

Lisa gently swatted him but smiled.

The waiter returned with the wine and after the usual ritual, poured each of them a glass and left the remainder in an ice bucket next to the table.

Lisa looked around. The restaurant was cozy and definitely upscale. She was glad she'd packed several dresses and that she'd found this one to match her needs for the evening. In the centre of the room was a round fireplace with a roaring fire inside making it even cosier.

Martin smiled at her and admired the ring on her finger. It fit perfectly and he admired the rest of her hand before he slid his over hers and gave a gentle squeeze.

The waiter brought their meals and they ate quietly and Martin finally asked what had Lisa up in the middle of the night.

She frowned at first remembering the list she'd made and smiled when she realized it was still in the pocket of her robe. "I was thinking about so many things but I wandered through the house and, despite it being dark, realized it would be the perfect place for a wedding reception."

Martin smiled. He was worried she was thinking about work or changing her mind. "I think it would work well too."

"I also had a dream the other night that we got married at sunset in the backyard," she told him.

Martin didn't comment this time. Instead, he closed his eyes and tried to picture it.

"You don't agree?" she asked. "I'm open to suggestions and it was only a dream after all."

Martin nodded and took another bite to eat. "I've been thinking too and I don't know what I'm going to do but I've been thinking of either selling the place, or closing it down as a B&B," he said.

Lisa was speechless for a moment. "I don't want you to have to do that because of me," she replied.

"It's not because of you, it would be because of 'us'," he said emphasizing the last word. "I love you and if you have to go back to your job, then I want to go with you," he said. "Plus, now that I have a companion, I wouldn't mind doing some traveling if you're game," he added.

Lisa nodded. "Travel where?" she asked, her interest now piqued.

"Anywhere you want to go but I was thinking of Europe, a cruise, whatever you like."

"I'd love to do all of those things," she began, "but I'd hate it if you gave all this up."

"How about we think about it and when we know better what's going on, we'll discuss it further," he suggested.

Lisa looked into his blue eyes and opened her mouth to say something but then closed it.

"What is it Lisa?" Martin pressed. "I know we haven't known each other for long but you *can* tell me anything."

"I was just thinking, what if you were to hire a manager for the place if we have to move? I have a place in K-W and my income more than covers the rent so you could still do both," she said.

Martin nodded. "I like that idea. It's definitely realistic."

Lisa smiled. It had taken courage but she'd said it.

After they finished eating, Martin led Lisa to the dance floor and pulled her close to him. He wrapped his arm tight around her yet held her hand as if it was porcelain. He led her expertly around the dance floor and Lisa was impressed.

"I love you Lisa," he began.

Lisa returned the sentiment and pressed her forehead against his shoulder. She had the start of a headache.

"I can't believe this," Martin continued.

"You've said that before," Lisa replied.

"I know I've said it before, but I still can't. If anyone would have told me the story I would never have believed it."

Now Lisa laughed. "Yeah, we're quite the pair. Neither of us believed in love at first sight until it struck us like a bolt of lightening."

"You have that analogy perfected," Martin replied. "You okay?" he asked.

Lisa shook her head. "I'm getting a headache," she told him.

"Excuse for tonight?" he asked with a smile.

Lisa shook her head. "No, I get migraines and I either ate something I shouldn't have or the weather is changing."

Martin leaned close to her and whispered in her ear, "the weather *is* changing, the forecast is calling for rain and thunderstorms tomorrow."

Lisa looked into his eyes. "I can tell."

"We'll leave as soon as this dance is over okay?" he asked.

Lisa nodded. She was glad she had brought her medication with her. It would be a lifesaver for her.

"Did you bring anything?" Martin asked.

Lisa nodded. "Yeah, I have some tablets in my cosmetic bag in our room."

The music stopped for a second and he led her to their table where she gathered her purse and he collected his receipt.

Martin took her hand and led her through the restaurant and out the door where the sky had clouded over with huge white clouds that almost glowed through the darkness. They walked the few minutes back and he held up a hand to Maria who wanted all the details of the evening.

"It's okay, I'll go up," Lisa told him and gave him a peck on the cheek.

"Are you sure?" he asked.

"I'll be fine, see you in a few minutes," she told him and let go of his hand and retreated upstairs.

"Is Miss Lisa not well?" Maria asked.

"No, she's not. She has a migraine and needs to take her medication," he explained.

"I'm so sorry," Maria said.

"It's okay, I feel bad that I was going to wave you off," he replied.

"I wouldn't have been offended knowing she's unwell," she said pointing towards the stairs.

"Anyway, it was a delightful evening. That place is just as beautiful as I remember it and the food is still delectable."

Maria nodded. "Yes, I haven't been in a while myself but once in a while Antoine will invite me over to try some of his new recipes," she said with a reminiscent air about her.

"I better go upstairs and check on Lisa," Martin told her.

Maria nodded but wouldn't let him go at that moment.

Martin hoped Lisa was okay and that she didn't need him for anything, even if it was a glass of water.

The first thing Lisa did when she got to the room was take her medication. She washed her face and brushed her teeth as well as changed out of her dress. She knew that within about 15 minutes she would be finding these activities a little more difficult as her blood vessels constricted in order to take away the migraine. She turned out the lights and stretched out on the bed willing the pain to go away and wondering where Martin was. She didn't want him around at the moment as she preferred to be alone at this point. Yet at the same time she wished he was with her, gently rubbing her back to help take her mind off the pain. She felt her heart start pumping harder and closed her eyes. She could almost feel the pain leave her body and she could feel her muscles relaxing also. Just then the lights went on.

"Oh God don't do that," she yelled.

"I'm sorry, I wasn't thinking," Martin said and he threw his jacket onto an armchair and went to her. He sat on the side of the bed beside her. "Oh God I'm so sorry, I really wasn't thinking," he said again.

"It's okay, really, it's starting to go away," she told him.

Martin got up and looked down at her. "Is it okay if I get ready for bed?" he asked.

"It's fine. Maria have lots to ask?" Lisa called to him in the bathroom.

"Yes, she wanted to know every detail," he called back.

Lisa could tell he was brushing his teeth as his response was garbled and she laughed in spite of how she was feeling.

He turned out the bathroom light and then the overhead light casting only shadows from outside across the room.

Lisa felt him get into bed beside her and she reached for him. "Can you please just hold me for a while?" she asked quietly through the darkness.

"Anything for you my darling, just say the word."

Lisa closed her eyes as his arms went around her and she could still feel her heart pounding working hard against the drugs.

Martin could feel it too and asked if she was really okay.

She explained what the medication did and why it was that her heart seemed to be pounding.

Martin didn't completely understand her but understood more than he had before. He kissed her neck and felt himself becoming aroused. He tried to will it away but it didn't work very well and automatically pressed himself against her.

Lisa felt it too and smiled through the darkness. "Please just wait a little longer," she said.

Martin took that as a good sign and left Lisa alone.

Lisa couldn't manage to stay awake any longer and as her eyes got heavier, she finally fell asleep.

Martin couldn't believe it. She had just told him to wait and now here she was sound asleep. He knew she'd wanted to make love. *Maybe it was just the medication,* he thought as he watched her sleep. He placed a hand over her heart and realized it had slowed way down. The little he knew about the human body told him that the pill she took would make her incredibly sleepy because the brain wouldn't have been getting enough oxygen. He suddenly felt like a heel but realized too late that his hand was over her breast too. He kissed her neck and nibbled at her earlobe. She felt wonderful in his arms and he wondered how many more nights they'd be able to spend this way.

Lisa moaned in her sleep and reached to place her hand over his at her breast. "Make love to me Martin," she whispered.

Martin helped remove her nightgown and eased her onto her back before he rose above her and entered her.

"Oh God Martin, you feel wonderful," she said into his ear before she nibbled there.

"You feel incredible, I don't know how much of this I can take," he replied.

Lisa lifted her hips to take in more of him.

Martin let nature take over which brought them both to a climax neither had experienced before. He pulled her into his arms and listened to her breathing heavily and regretted what they'd done. "I'm sorry, I shouldn't have put your body through that," he told her.

"On the contrary, it was wonderful," Lisa panted.

"I agree, but still," he said again. "Go to sleep."

Lisa did as she was told and looked forward to waking in the morning and returning to what was for now, her home.

CHAPTER 10

The next morning Lisa woke early feeling better but knew she wasn't out of the woods yet. She looked outside and saw it was extremely overcast and she knew by the end of the day she'd have another headache. She decided to fill the tub and have a hot soak rather than a shower.

It was as she was resting her head back that she had company and it was Martin's hands on her breasts that made her finally open her eyes.

"Morning beautiful, how are you feeling?" he asked despite having a feeling he knew exactly how she was feeling and the answer was not what he wanted to hear.

"I'm going to have another headache by the end of the day," she told him. "It looks awful outside and I can feel it hovering," she said as she twisted a wet hand over her head like it was a cloud.

"I'm sorry," he told her. "Is there anything I can do?"

Lisa shook her head. "Not really, I *could* take another of my pills but I could just as easily go downstairs for breakfast and a cup of tea and feel better too."

Martin didn't entirely understand but he nodded in understanding. He stood and slipped into the tub with her, holding her and eventually he helped to wash her hair and sponge her down before she got out and towelled off while he watched. Then it was her turn to sit on the side of the tub and chat with him.

They dressed and went downstairs where they found Maria waiting for them in the dining room.

"Come in, sit, I'll get you breakfast," she said. Then she stopped on her way to the kitchen. "How are you feeling?" she asked Lisa.

"I'm okay," Lisa told her. "Very tired."

Maria nodded and left the room only to return a few moments later with a steaming pot of coffee and two plates of eggs, bacon, toast and pancakes.

Lisa looked at all the food and felt awful that there was no way she was going to be able to eat all this. She was lucky if she got a bowl of cereal for breakfast most mornings and despite having been with Martin for the last three mornings, he had gone easy with breakfast. "Could I have a cup of tea please, Maria?" she asked.

Maria nodded. "Most certainly, I will be right back." Again she left the room and Lisa turned to look at Martin, her eyes bulging.

"I'm never going to eat all this," she told him. "Especially after last night."

"Eat what you can, it'll help you in the long run I'm sure," he told her.

She nodded and started eating slowly, talking quietly.

"I'd still like to finish shopping this morning," Lisa told him.

"I'd love to go with you," he replied. "If that's okay," he added quickly not wanting to get in her way.

Lisa nodded and by that time Maria had returned with her tea and she took a sip and savoured it for a few moments as it settled in her stomach and seemed to fill her all over with some relief.

They finished breakfast and told Maria they would be going back to their room to pack.

"Is it okay if we leave our bags here so we can finish shopping?" Martin asked.

"That's no problem at all. My home is yours for as long as you need it," Maria replied with a smile.

They gave her a smile before going upstairs and packing up most of their belongings.

Lisa wanted to make love with Martin but she also wanted to go shopping and get back *home*. There she could perhaps seduce him and they could spend the afternoon or evening doing so.

They finished packing in good time and, after dropping their luggage with Maria, walked out the door holding hands.

It was a couple of hours later when they returned, arms full of packages. Martin was relieved he hadn't packed the car yet as there were a few items that would need to be packed carefully to avoid breakage.

They hugged Maria goodbye and she wished them well, not only for the drive, but also their nuptials, whenever they would take place. She also reminded them to keep her in mind for her catering services and they promised that they would.

The drive back felt shorter and Lisa was really feeling the headache coming on again and she excused herself as soon as they got back. Unfortunately, probably because of the car ride, she was very nauseous and by the time she got upstairs to the bathroom, she hardly had time to kneel before the dry heaves started, then she finally threw up. "Oh God," she called out from the pain in her throat.

"What's wrong?" Martin called bursting through the bathroom door and seeing her on the floor in front of the toilet. "Oh darling," he said as he fell to his knees next to her. He pulled her into his arms the best he could but it wasn't much help as she leaned forward again and vomited a little more. He reached for some tissue and handed it to her.

Lisa took it from him and started to cry. The pain was intense and she knew she'd let it go far too long this time. "I'm sorry."

"For what? For throwing up? That's absurd, I won't hear of it," he told her. "Are you finished though?" he asked.

She nodded and he helped her to stand. He could feel her trembling and he led her into the bedroom and helped her out of her shoes as she laid back. "Can I get you anything?" he asked.

She nodded again and told him to bring her cosmetic bag from their trip and a glass of water.

Martin left the room and said a small prayer for her wellbeing. He found the bag and took the stairs two at a time to the top. He handed it to her and went into the bathroom to get her the water.

Lisa found her pill bottle at the bottom of the bag and, after fumbling to get the cap off, slid a small, orange tablet onto her tongue. She closed her eyes and waited for it to dissolve.

Martin came in and stood at the side of the bed and waited for her to open her eyes. She finally did and she took the water and took a sip.

"Did you take your medication?" he asked.

She nodded. "They dissolve so I just need a little water to wash down the taste of it."

Martin looked at her, his eyes full of deep concern for her. "I want you to stay here and rest, sleep, whatever you need to do."

She nodded and rolled over onto her side and listened as Martin left the room.

Martin returned downstairs and looked at all the luggage in the foyer. He decided he'd put it temporarily in the room where Lisa had started out in and he'd get a few things done himself.

It was several hours later when Lisa woke. She felt like she had a hangover and she was slightly disoriented. She looked around the room and then took inventory of her headache. It was gone as was the nausea but she was also very hungry. She sucked in a deep breath and sat up slowly. She waited for the wave of dizziness to pass before she stood, then went to the bathroom. She splashed some cool water on her face and used the toilet before she went back to the bedroom and sat back on all the pillows again just as Martin came in.

"How are you feeling? Do you need anything?" he asked.

Lisa nodded. "I'm okay, but I'm hungry," she told him.

Martin left the room without another word and returned within five minutes with toast, crackers and weak tea and told her there was a pot of soup heating up.

She smiled at him as she took a sip of the tea and then took a bite of the toast. When she'd finished, he took the tray from her and went to check on the soup and brought her a bowl.

"Listen, I'm going to go downstairs and start making some supper. I'll keep it light okay?"

Lisa nodded and decided she wasn't going anywhere else tonight with how she was feeling. "Could you bring me my bags please?" she asked.

He nodded as he left the room and returned in a moment with the bags that were hers. "Here you are," he told her.

She sat up again, taking it easy once more, and went to them. As he went downstairs, she unpacked her things and when she came across it, she set the nightgown aside, finished unpacking and then slid into the nightgown. It was pure heaven and she slid under the covers and curled up, easily slipping back into the sleep from whence she'd come not that long ago.

Later, after she'd been woken by Martin, she sat up too quickly and was dizzy once more and reached for her head.

Again terror shot through Martin as he watched her and he cursed the weather and whatever else was causing his fiancée to feel this horrible.

"I'm okay," she assured him.

He held her close and then helped her out of bed and into her bathrobe. He wasn't certain of the stairs with her but with someone to lean on, she manoeuvred them just fine. He got her sitting down in the dining room, where he had lit the candles and turned out the lights, before he retrieved an easy casserole from the kitchen and carried it in.

They ate in almost silence, Martin's concern for her almost unbearable.

"I'll be okay, I've been through this before," Lisa finally said, trying to assure him.

"How do you do it?" he asked.

"It doesn't usually get this bad but once in a while I don't get to it fast enough and it gets away from me," she explained.

Later on, Martin carried her off to bed where they very gently made love and he held onto her extra tight for the entire night, waking frequently to check on her. It was sometime around sunrise when he finally drifted into a deep sleep.

CHAPTER 11

Lisa woke first the next morning and was very groggy from the headache and meds she'd taken the day before. She slid out of bed, tiptoed to the bathroom and then out of the bedroom down to the kitchen where she made breakfast for herself and then proceeded to make something for Martin and carried it up to him. She set it on the small table and walked over to the bed where Martin was sprawled on his stomach snoring very softly. She leaned down close to his ear and whispered. "Morning sexy."

"Mmmm, oh, how are you feeling?" he asked.

"I'm fine," she replied. "I've had some breakfast, I'm on the mend. I brought you some," she told him waving her hand in the general direction of the table.

"I'd rather have you," he told her and put his arm around her and pulled her close.

She leaned down and kissed him before she stood up, took her nighty off and straddled him.

"I like this I think," he said as he reached up and caressed her breasts. Soon breakfast was forgotten and they were making love.

When they had both climaxed, Martin waited until he had caught his breath. "I think I could go for some coffee now," he said.

Lisa giggled. *I could go for a nap,* she thought and closed her eyes.

Martin got up and went to the table where he took a sip of the coffee and then set it down and went to the bathroom.

Lisa heard him close the door but it seemed distant and felt great just being able to relax with her eyes closed.

Martin returned to the bedroom and went for more coffee. He turned to her and called her name softly and she didn't stir. He smiled, took a sip and went and had a shower. *She needs her rest so I'll get a few things done,* he thought while the hot water ran over him.

He pulled the covers over Lisa and went downstairs with the tray. After cleaning the kitchen up, he went outside and started moving some more of his firewood around as he would soon be getting his winter order. His thoughts turned to Lisa while he worked and the predicament she was in. The uncertainty of her future and even his own. He knew there were years between them but his love for her was certain. He didn't want to give up the B&B but would if he had to because he loved her so much and that's all that really mattered to him. He never knew he would find love twice in his lifetime and despite having been married to someone he loved, this was far different. The feelings between them were inexplicable and he could only look to a higher power. *Of all the B&Bs, how did she end up at mine?* What had drawn her here? But is there something that could drive her away too? One negative piece of advice from a friend or family member could have her retreating. He *had* to show her that his love for her was real. He didn't know how he was going to do that, to create an environment that she would feel welcome in and that she would want to stay in. But he was also willing to give it all up and move back to the city with her if that's what it took.

Lord help me, he began to pray. *Help me keep her in my life, that's all I want. I know she knows I love her but is that enough? I have never loved anyone as much as I love her and I feel like You brought her to me. So help me be patient and help both of us make the right decisions.*

He sighed and hauled the last bundle of wood.

He was taking his gloves off and was about to wash his hands in the kitchen when he heard the water running upstairs. He went quietly up the stairs and poked his head into the bedroom. There was no sign of Lisa and he assumed she was in the shower. He debated on going in but thought he would leave her alone for now and went back downstairs where he put the kettle on for tea.

Lisa stood under the water in the shower and couldn't help thinking. She thought of all the things she needed to do now that she was back and her mind turned to her list. She was definitely going to borrow the phone and internet and get some input from people, at least see where she stood with her parents and family.

She shut the water off and dried off. Her thoughts turned to Martin and she wondered what he was doing and was startled a short time later to find him in the kitchen with a pot of tea.

"Would you like a cup?" he asked.

Lisa nodded and sat at the breakfast bar. "I'd love some," she replied. "What have you been up to?" she asked.

"Just moving around my firewood since I'm due for some more," he told her.

He carried a cup over to her and set it down in front of her. "Here you are. Did you enjoy your nap?" he asked.

"I didn't think I was actually that tired yet," she told him. "But I guess I was."

Then Martin told her he had been thinking while he was moving the wood and he couldn't help but reassure her that he was more than willing to move back to the city for her. He didn't go into detail but he told her his fears as well.

"Listen, I don't know exactly what's going to happen or how people are going to react. I can't help but to be uncertain right now. I'm so torn between wanting to go back and wanting to stay here. I want to make some phone calls and send some emails today. I need to get a few things started."

Martin nodded. It was all he really needed to hear at this point. He was happy to know she wasn't being unreasonable and that she was trying to compromise as much as he was. "I'll let you get to that, my computer is in the den so feel free to use it. There's also a phone in there."

Lisa thanked him with a kiss on the cheek and took her tea with her.

Martin watched her go and thought he'd go back outside and check on a few other things. Then he realized he needed to get something ready for lunch and stayed inside working quietly in the kitchen.

Lisa called her parents first. She talked to her dad first and was congratulated on her news. Her mother, on the other hand, was full of mean things to say to her. She wanted to know all the details and even progressed to asking if Lisa was drunk when she'd agreed to marrying the host of the B&B she's staying at.

Lisa was near tears and she told her mother she was cruel and that she had to go because she was going to be looking for a job locally. That got her mother going again about never being able to see her and Lisa finally found the courage to tell her mother that perhaps she would *actually* prefer it that way.

It was a half hour later when she got off the phone and she rested her head on the desk and cried. On one hand at least she knew where her mother stood but at the same time she was upset because she wanted her mother's support in all of this.

"Are you okay?" Martin asked as he came rushing into the room. "What's wrong? What happened?" he asked.

Lisa lifted her head off the desk and let him cradle her in his arms. Between sobs, she filled him in on what had been said to her.

Martin thought it was damn rude of her mother to say those things to her and he told her so.

"I'm not just upset about her saying it, I'm also angry because I really wanted her to be happy for me especially after all the years she's spent harping at me."

Martin only nodded and rubbed her back. Then the phone rang. He picked it up and prepared himself for who it might be. "Hello?" he said more gruffly than he had intended in case it was a customer. He listened intently for a few moments before he told the caller to hold on a moment. "It's your dad," he said to Lisa.

Lisa took the phone and sobbed a hello. She listened and said 'uh-huh' a lot before she finally thanked him for calling and hung up. She turned to Martin who was looking at her quizzically. "He apologized for my mother's behaviour. He thinks my news is great and he's going to talk to her and talk her into being more open about it."

Martin thought that was great and told her so. "Come have some lunch," he said and helped her out of the chair.

Lisa and Martin had a quiet lunch as Lisa finally stopped crying. "I think I'll take a walk after lunch," she told him.

"Care for some company?" Martin asked.

Lisa shook her head. "No, I'm going to do this one on my own."

Martin nodded. He thought he understood but he wasn't sure.

She checked her email online and then went to the internal job postings. There was nothing there for this area at this time and she proceeded to go for her walk.

She headed to the beach but it was a cold, overcast day and she wasn't there for very long before it started to rain. She almost ran back to the house and ran right into Martin as she went through the door.

"Whoa!" he said as he held her at arms length for a moment. "Get caught in the rain?" he asked.

"Yeah, where did that come from so fast?" she asked.

"It does that when you're near the lake," he explained. "Come on, let's get you out of these wet clothes." He took her hand and led her upstairs where he undressed her and stretched out on the bed beside her where he made love to her.

They cuddled and decided to retreat to the den where Martin built a fire and got out an old poetry book of his and he read to her as she giggled at him with the voices he was using.

"I didn't know you liked poetry," she said.

"There's a lot you don't know about me," Martin said. "That's why we are going to spend the rest of our lives getting to know each other," he added.

Lisa smiled and he continued to read.

"Oh, I like that one," Lisa said about a poem about love.

Martin nodded, "I like it too," he told her. "Do you know any card games?" he asked.

"I know how to play crib," she told him.

"Really?" Martin asked shocked she would know.

"Yeah, my parents taught me how to play, it's my favourite."

"Are you up for a game?" he asked.

"You bet," she said. "I'm just going to use the bathroom."

"I'll make a pot of tea," he added.

Lisa nodded and got up, leaving the room while Martin did the same.

Lisa made it back to the den first and stood in front of the fire for a few minutes before she went over to the computer and logged back into her email. She had no reply from Gerry yet and wondered what was taking so long. But then she wondered what she expected, him to give her an answer right away?

She sat back down and waited for Martin to bring in the tea and helped him lower the tray to the floor when he did.

He went to a cupboard next to the fireplace and pulled out the crib board and a deck of cards.

They played for the rest of the afternoon and Martin left her to make them some dinner. Lisa thought some more about everything that was happening, all that was going on and all that would be going on. Her thoughts, without her control, turned to possible wedding plans and that made her smile. She rested her head back and closed her eyes trying to picture what it was she was looking for in a gown. She couldn't picture anything specific, she just knew she wanted something big. *It's a start*, she thought.

"What are you thinking?" Martin asked as he placed a kiss on her neck.

"I'm just thinking of a few wedding ideas," she told him.

"Oh really? Like what?"

"I was thinking about what I might want to wear."

"I think you will look terrific in anything," he said as he sat down beside her and put his arms around her.

"Thanks," she leaned over and kissed him on the cheek.

Martin allowed her to kiss him on the cheek before he turned his face to her and kissed her full on the mouth.

She let him scoop her up and carry her upstairs where they made love.

"What happened to supper?" Lisa asked.

"It's cooking," Martin assured her. "It'll be ready shortly. Is it okay that we started with dessert?" he asked.

"It's perfectly fine as long as we can still have dessert after too," she told him.

"We most certainly can," he told her.

They only put their robes on and Martin decided to serve supper in the den so he went in and added another log to the fire before he went to the kitchen to check on supper.

Lisa followed him in and took some dishes from the cupboards. She carried them to the den and set the coffee table. She rounded up a few pillows and put them on the floor to sit on.

"Here's the wine," Martin said carrying in a bottle and two glasses.

Lisa took them from him and filled each of the glasses. She looked around the room and realized there were a few candles around so she turned out the lights and lit the candles. She placed two on the coffee table and the room was lit by just the fireplace and the candles. It looked absolutely wonderful and Martin said just that as he carried dinner into the room.

"Thanks, I thought something different would be nice," she explained.

"I think it looks wonderful," he said again and he served up dinner.

They ate quietly, both deep in thought about their separate futures and their future together.

Martin cleared away the dinner dishes and carried in dessert that he began serving by feeding it to her.

Lisa took it from him but also made a point of licking his finger as well.

Martin narrowed his eyes and looked at her with seduction on his face. He pulled her to the floor and untied her bathrobe. He slid his hand inside and cupped her breast before he rose and went to retrieve a few of the pillows so they could lie in front of the fire in comfort. Once they'd settled back in, Martin returned to nibbling at her breast and it wasn't long before he was inside her.

Lisa was so relaxed that she closed her eyes and just let herself go.

Martin was only a little surprised that Lisa had fallen asleep on him. She was tired and he just continued to gently stroke her hand as he held it and his own mind started to wander. He wondered how on earth he could be this active sexually when he was as old as he was. He felt like a teenager just aware of his hormones for the first time. His mind surged forward into the future and he suddenly wondered about children. Would Lisa want to have a baby? Does Lisa want kids? What about his going before her? What would that do? He had never given a single thought to those things ahead of time but knew that when you're thinking with your heart you tend to not think of other things—like logic. He chuckled to himself and made a mental note to ask Lisa about that in the morning. He also wondered where they would live. He'd love to live here but he didn't know how Lisa felt about that and it depended on her job and where that took them. He realized he really was willing to go where ever it was she needed him and he smiled. If they stayed here, he wasn't sure if he wanted this to remain a B&B especially if they decided to have kids. This was too hard to deal with. Maybe he should forget it all. He looked down at her face—so content, so peaceful and he noticed a tiny smile across her lips and he realized he couldn't. This wasn't a schoolboy crush, this was true love, it might have happened fast, but it was definitely love... pure and simple.

He got up carefully, put the fire out and then very gently picked her up off the floor and carried her upstairs to bed. It was hard to tuck her in without reaching out to touch her as he had carried her up here with nothing on.

He had to go back downstairs to turn out the lights and after he'd turned off the last one he thought he saw something glowing in the corner of the den. He didn't know much about these things but he said hello to it and it seemed to glow brighter and then fade some.

"Who are you?" he asked.

The light did nothing and Martin didn't know what else to say to it. He figured he'd tell Lisa about it in the morning and perhaps they could research together. He didn't realize what Lisa had said was true about the house being haunted. It's not like he was handed a manual when he bought the place. "Is there something I can do for you?" he asked as if it were a customer. A piece of paper shot through the air and he caught it just as the light grew brighter and then disappeared like a bolt of lightening.

Martin turned the light back on and looked at the paper. It appeared to be a map of some kind but it wasn't to scale that was for sure. There was also letters on it *SL*. He didn't know what that was. Initials? The start of a word? He would have to work on it in the morning.

He dragged himself off to bed, leaving the paper lying on the desk. He thought about it until he finally fell asleep.

CHAPTER 12

Someone was calling. Martin couldn't see who it was but it sounded like Lisa. There was a lot of noise though, like water. The waves, he thought finally cluing in. What's Lisa doing in the water? It's too cold to swim. He got out of bed and started looking for her. He looked out the bedroom window and could barely make out a form in the moonlight. It was a cold night and the wind was picking up, what was she thinking? He ran through the house and heard the baby crying in the background. It seemed he could never quite get to the kitchen. It was a struggle. He was panting by the time he got to the kitchen door and sucked in a deep breath when he opened the door and the wind caught him. He ran across the lawn which again was wider than he thought and he could hear the calling get louder and it seemed to be carried on the wind.

"Lisa!" he called back to her. "What are you doing?"

There was no answer and he looked down from the top of the steps and saw nobody. He felt a heavy feeling in his gut that something had gone wrong and he tore down the stairs almost falling twice before he got to the bottom. He tripped through the sand which was heavy and weighed down from the water spraying off the lake. He looked both ways and out as far as he could and didn't see anyone.

"I love you," he heard on the wind.

"I love you too, what are you doing?" he called back but got no answer again.

"Wake up," Lisa was shaking him. She wondered what was wrong with him. He had been shouting her name and wrestling with the covers. "Martin, I love you too," she told him. "But you have to wake up."

Martin didn't want to leave the beach but somebody was calling him back. He wondered if Lisa had doubled back to the house. He started to stir and finally opened his eyes. "Lisa!" he said.

"Yes, I'm here," she told him. "I'm right here, where have you been?"

"At the beach, you were there, you had been walking out into the water, it's windy, the waves," he went on and on.

"Calm down, you've been in bed, I've been in bed," she assured him.

Martin looked around the room. He wasn't sure what was happening at the moment and he reached out and hugged Lisa.

Lisa hugged him back and wondered again what it was he may have been dreaming about. "We'll make sense of it in the morning okay?" she tried to reassure him some more.

Martin nodded and kissed her. He held her extra close after they made love and it took him a while to fall back to sleep but he managed and slept until morning.

Lisa got out of bed first, a little shaken about what had happened in the middle of the night. She wasn't sure what to make of Martin's outburst and she walked down to the kitchen and started making coffee.

While it was brewing, she walked through to the den and smiled as she remembered their lovemaking the night before. She noticed the piece of paper on the desk and picked it up. She carried it back to the kitchen, studying it, trying to figure out what it meant. The letters *SL* where the only letters on the whole sheet and the rest looked like a map of something, like someone was trying to tell somebody something. She shrugged her shoulders and set the paper on the breakfast bar while she proceeded to put together some breakfast.

"Morning," Martin said as he entered the kitchen. He walked over to her and gave her a hug from behind and kissed her neck.

"Mmm, that was yummy," Lisa said.

"It certainly was," Martin replied. "Need help?" he asked.

"Nope, it's just about done," she said referring to the pot of oatmeal she was stirring.

Martin sat on one of the stools. "You found the piece of paper?" he asked.

Lisa turned to look at him and then nodded. "What is it?" she asked.

"You're guess is as good as mine," Martin told her. "You'll never guess where it came from and I'm afraid you'll think I'm losing my mind if I tell you," he went on.

Lisa looked at him. "Now you're scaring me," she told him.

"Last night I carried you up to bed and then I came back down to turn out the lights," he started.

Lisa scooped oatmeal out of the pot into two bowls and set one before him. She nodded for him to continue.

"Thank you," he said pointing his spoon at his breakfast. "There was a glow in the corner of the den," he stopped to take a bite of food.

Lisa was eating but unaware of it at that moment.

"This piece of paper shot out of it. I remembered you saying about the place being haunted and I think they're trying to tell us something," he said quickly.

Lisa smiled. "So it didn't say anything, or do anything?" she asked.

"No, it sat there. It got brighter for a second when I said hello to it, as if saying hello back."

Lisa looked again at the piece of paper. "What is this though?" She turned it around in all different directions.

"I have no idea," he replied. "I don't even know what the letters *SL* stand for."

"Do you mind if I spend a bit of time working on it?" she asked.

"Not at all, in fact I thought we could work on it together."

Lisa smiled. "Ghosthunters, in it together," she teased.

They finished their breakfast and it was as Martin was putting the dishes into the dishwasher that Lisa gasped. "Your dream, do you remember any of it?" she asked.

"Not really, well, maybe," he replied slowly.

"What was it about?" she pressed.

"I was running, it was you, you were in the water. It was dark. You were calling to me from the lake," he told her. "I got out of bed, I was trying to save you, the baby was crying," he told her.

"The baby? What baby?" Lisa asked.

"I don't know. Your baby? Our baby? There was definitely a baby, or I thought of there being a baby," he told her. "Maybe that was because I was thinking of asking you about having babies this morning."

Lisa opened her mouth then closed it. "You were? You were going to ask me about having a baby?"

Martin nodded. "Yeah, I was doing some thinking last night and I realized I don't even know if you want kids and thought I'd ask you this morning," he admitted sheepishly.

Lisa put her arms around him. "Yes, I want to have kids," she replied. Then she kissed him hard on the mouth for a moment before softening the kiss and running her tongue around his lips forcing his lips to open.

"Oh God I love you," Martin whispered as he pulled her to the floor.

"I love you too," Lisa replied as her bathrobe was parted and Martin's hands started caressing her, a finger sliding deep inside her.

Martin didn't take too long before he entered her, taking in how warm it felt to be there, how very close he felt to her and how damn lucky he felt to have had this woman walk into his life.

They propped themselves up against the cupboards after they'd climaxed and Martin breathed in the scent of Lisa's hair.

They showered together and Lisa went downstairs to the den where there were built-in bookshelves filled with books that Martin had said came with the house along with a lot of the furnishings. Martin had to meet the delivery guy with the firewood and had gone outside to make sure nothing had happened to shift the wood he'd moved a few days earlier. Lisa thought the collection was fabulous but after looking through the titles realized that most of what was here was just an old collection of first edition books that someone had taken great care of.

She thought of entering the initials into a search engine on the internet but figured that would turn up so many answers she'd never find what she was looking for anyway. So she sat in front of the fireplace and stared at the piece of paper turning it slowly.

Suddenly she jumped off the couch and ran upstairs. But she wasn't sure what she was looking for and she went into every room on that floor. She turned the paper just so and she checked all the closets but it still didn't completely make sense.

"Lisa?" Martin called to her from downstairs.

"Yeah," she called back.

"Where are you?" he asked as he mounted the stairs and stood at the top looking back and forth.

"I'm looking for something," she called back before she poked her head out of the room at the far end of the hall opposite their bedroom.

"Like what?" he asked.

She showed him the map again. "I think this is the layout of the house," she explained running her fingernail around the outer edge. "And I think these are windows," she explained pointing to tiny, almost invisible markings on the paper.

"Wait a second," he told her and examined it for a few seconds longer. "Come with me," he said and grabbed her hand almost dragging her down the stairs.

"Where are we going?" she asked as she stumbled trying to keep up.

Martin led her out the front door and kept walking.

"Where are we going?" she asked.

"Just a second," Martin said. He kept looking over his shoulder and then stopped, Lisa crashing into him.

"Whoa," she said.

"Sorry," he replied and pulled her into his arms. "Look," he said pointing up to windows above the second story of the house.

"What's that?" she asked.

"It would be a third floor of some kind," he told her. "Maybe just an attic."

"But how do we get up there?" she asked.

He shrugged. "I don't know. I've never looked for a door. Isn't that awful?"

Lisa shrugged this time. It was kind of awful because it was his house but then again, if there was no visible access then why would he bother even thinking about it.

Just as they were about to go back inside, a truck pulled into the laneway.

"You go ahead," Martin said, "I'm going to be a while."

"Any suggestions on where I should start looking?" she asked.

Martin shook his head. "I'm not sure," he replied.

Lisa went back inside and was grateful because it was a little cool outside without a jacket. Just as she got inside she had a second thought though and grabbed her jacket and went back outside, this time out through the kitchen to the back. She walked almost as far as the top of the stairs to the beach before she could see and she studied the top floor of the house trying to determine where the access point may be. A fleeting thought left her wondering if the blueprints were anywhere in the house including those from any renovations that were done. She had one last look and went back inside glad that she had grabbed her jacket this time. She went back to the den and looked through the volumes of books again uncertain where she might find something like that. She noticed the one shelf had doors on it and she opened one to discover that there were rolls of paper inside. *Jackpot,* she thought as she read the slanted writing on the yellowing paper. *I'll start with this one,* she thought and pulled one out.

It was just what she was looking for, however she had no idea how to read these things. She looked at one that said *Foundation* and instantly turned the page. The blueprints increased by floor so she flipped to the one of the *Second Floor.* She saw that the original plan had been changed quite a bit with the renovations and saw that part of the hallway had been open where there was now a room. She examined the entire page until she found a set of stairs separate to those that led to the second floor. She picked this page out of the pile and went upstairs trying to picture how the walls would have been but found it somewhat difficult to interpret.

She returned to the den and pulled another roll out of the cupboard, this one with a different year on it and spread it out on the desk. These were the ones she needed as they were from the first set of renovations that were done. She lined it up next to the original blueprint and looked back and forth between the two. She found the stairs on the second set of blueprints and sucked in a breath. She pulled this page from the stack and followed it like a map once she got to the top of the stairs. She went left down the hallway almost to the end and turned left into the room over the front of the house. She had to turn around a few times before she realized that the wardrobe stood in the way of what she wanted. She tried to look in behind but it was impossible, she'd have to wait for Martin to help her and she wasn't even sure he'd be able to because wardrobes were generally really heavy. She wondered who would have closed this off. She opened the door of the wardrobe and noticed that there had been a door cut into the back of it. She tried to open it but it wouldn't work. She figured that someone had had good intentions at the time but it hadn't worked. She had an idea and went downstairs and out the front door.

"Hey sweetie, what's up?" Martin asked as he helped the wood guy pile up some of the wood along the side of the house.

"I found the door I think, but it's behind a wardrobe. I thought maybe you could get Todd to help you move it before he leaves," she explained.

Martin went back to working and Lisa could hear him asking for help moving a piece of furniture. She watched as

Martin received a nod in return and after blowing him a kiss she went back inside to start making some lunch.

It wasn't long after that Martin and Todd came into the house and she led them upstairs to the room. Martin wasn't certain about it until Lisa showed him the blueprints and then the door in the back of the wardrobe. He and Todd didn't hesitate any longer and went about moving the wardrobe away from the wall far enough so they could gain access to whatever it was that was behind.

Todd collected his cheque and went on his way wishing them luck with what they'd just uncovered.

Lisa told Martin she'd made them lunch and that they should eat first before they began this new adventure.

Martin agreed and they talked about what it was she'd found which they both agreed was access to an attic. They also agreed that they weren't certain how long ago it had been covered by the wardrobe and Martin felt horrible that he'd never come across it or made any realization that there were windows above those on the second floor which must belong to something.

"I guess I just figured they were attached to venting or something," he said sheepishly.

Lisa smiled. "Don't beat yourself up over it, you haven't been here that long, you were bound to realize it sooner or later."

Martin nodded and wiped his mouth on his napkin, drank the last of the hot chocolate she'd made for him because she knew he'd be cold after spending all that time outside, and stood up. He helped clear the dishes into the dishwasher and took Lisa's hand. He led her upstairs and back down to the bedroom where they looked at each other before Martin gingerly pulled on the door handle and it creaked on its rusted hinges.

The blueprints had been right, there was a staircase leading to another level of the house and they carefully climbed up aware that there may be worn or weak boards. At the top they both gasped, not only from the dust in the air but from the scene before them. Trunks and boxes were scattered everywhere. Lisa took the small piece of paper from her pocket and noticed that the layout of the attic was an exact match to the drawing. There was a small dot on one of the squares in the drawing and she realized now that it must be an 'X' not actually a dot.

"This must be what we're supposed to look for," she told Martin and pointed at the dot on the paper.

"But look at all this stuff," Martin said. "I can't believe it. Where did it all come from?"

"*Who* does it all belong to?" Lisa asked.

Martin shrugged. "I don't know any of the history of this house," he explained.

Lisa began walking through the maze towards the 'X' on the map and stopped in front of a trunk that seemed to have been wiped clean of its dust and the letters *SL* stared up at them from the brass plate on the lid. "S-L," Lisa exclaimed.

Martin joined her and still couldn't figure out what was at play here and he wasn't sure he wanted to know either. He wasn't afraid of the paranormal but he'd never experienced it in his own life and preferred to leave it on TV.

Lisa was fascinated and tried to lift the lid. It was only after she couldn't that Martin noticed the padlock that held it.

Lisa turned to look at Martin with a 'what now' look on her face and frowned as Martin shrugged his shoulders.

Lisa examined the map more closely and didn't find anything else marked on it. "Maybe we should take it downstairs with us," she suggested. "Try using a hammer or something to pry it open?" she queried hoping for some guidance from Martin.

"Yeah, if we take it down I can get out a number of tools to try and get into it," he replied.

They lifted it and were surprised it was lighter than they had both anticipated. They decided to carry it down to the main floor so that it could be cleaned off and opened in the kitchen.

Once they set it down on the floor, Martin went to find some tools he thought might work to open it and Lisa sat down wondering what might be in it. She also wondered if any of it had to do with Martin's dream.

"Wondering what's in there?" Martin asked when he returned.

Lisa nodded. "Hard to believe what it could be."

Martin started with the crowbar figuring leverage would pop the lock open easily after all these years.

"It's not going to work is it?" Lisa asked.

Martin shook his head. "No, I think I'm going to have to shatter it with the hammer, or hopefully," he replied reaching for the hammer and a screwdriver. "Stand back, I don't know what's going to happen when I give this thing a good whack."

Lisa stood on the other side of the island while Martin inserted the screwdriver into the large keyhole in the lock and gave it a few good whacks with the hammer. It cracked and then fell off the trunk.

"Oh my God, you got in," Lisa said quietly. She didn't know why she was nervous about this, she knew nothing about what would be found inside but she found herself anticipating it at the same time.

"You want the honours?" Martin asked after he'd cleaned away the lock.

Lisa was going to shake her head but she changed her mind and nodded instead. She walked around the island and towards the trunk. She took a deep breath before she slowly bent over to release the latch and felt heat emanating from it. She slipped the latch and pulled the lid up.

Martin helped her to flip the lid back and they looked down to what was inside.

"Most of it is just clothing," Lisa said a little disappointed. She reached inside and pulled out a beautiful gown. Beneath that were more pieces of cloth, well preserved over the years probably by what had approximated to a case of moth balls.

Martin pulled out stacks of the clothing and uncovered a jewellery box in the bottom. "We might have something here," he told her.

Lisa reached in and gently pulled it out and set it on the table. She bent the lid back and they looked inside. Nested there was a velvet ring box which Martin reached in and picked up. He opened the lid and the hinge broke so he set it aside and they looked at the diamond ring that lay inside. It was quite splendid and Lisa gasped when she saw it.

They ended up rifling through everything in the jewellery box as well as what remained in the trunk and tucked in the very bottom was a stack of love letters. "I wonder if these will help us figure out who she was," she said as she untied the string that held them tight and unfolded the first one.

> *To my dearest Sophia,*
> *I can't say how much I enjoyed our first meeting. You may not believe this but I think I fell in love with you the first time I laid eyes on you. Your beauty left me almost speechless so I find myself writing this letter to ask if you would be interested in seeing me again. Perhaps we could go to the theatre on Saturday evening?*
> *Love,*

Isaac

"This is incredible," Lisa said. "The letter is dated May 2, 1920."

"Now you know where to start," Martin said referring to her wish to research what had happened so many years ago.

"This is fantastic."

Martin smiled at her. He was glad she was finally cheering up a bit. She'd been here almost a week and despite their relationship, he hadn't seen her happy about too much else.

They picked everything up and moved it into the dining room item by item. When Lisa picked up one of the folded nightgowns, she was surprised when something fell out of it.

Martin bent over and picked it up and they examined it. It was a small silver baby carriage.

"It's beautiful," Lisa said taking it in her palm. "There must have been a baby," she said.

"Maybe there was a baby on the way," Martin suggested.

"Are you saying perhaps she lost it?" Lisa asked.

Martin shrugged. "I don't know," he replied.

Lisa looked at him. "It's kind of fun to speculate isn't it?"

Martin nodded and then leaned down and kissed her. He was turned on by her excitement over this new find and he pulled her close to him.

"Make love to me," Lisa almost begged.

Martin didn't need to hear anymore and he scooped her off the floor and carried her upstairs. He set her down on the bed and very slowly removed her clothes. He kissed her from head to toe and brought her to climax a number of times before he rose above her and entered her.

There was a newfound passion between them and Martin knew it had something to do with their newest find but then he realized it was more the excitement it brought to Lisa that was truly changing.

"Oh Martin, you feel incredible," Lisa said as she held him, her legs winding around him to pull him closer to her.

It wasn't long before Martin was climaxing and trying desperately to catch his breath.

After he'd caught his breath, he snuck a glimpse at his watch and realized it was well past time to make a decent dinner. "Get dressed in one of those fancy dresses, I'm taking you out for dinner," he told Lisa.

Lisa smiled and then rolled over. "Okay, same place or somewhere different?" she asked.

"The same, sorry but the town's too small to have many options," he replied.

"I know, I just thought I'd ask," she told him and giggled.

They showered together and Lisa got dressed, feeling very lucky she had shopped in the store she'd found in Bayfield. This time she chose the purple velvet dress she'd found there and was told that was the colour of the season. She slid her feet into her pumps and went downstairs where she found Martin fumbling to open a catch on a necklace.

"For me?" she asked.

Martin blushed. "Yeah, I was trying to be a little more graceful than this though," he told her. "I found this and thought of you."

"Where did you find it?" she asked.

"I found it in Bayfield when you went off on your little shopping excursion and I went on mine."

She smiled and thanked him with a kiss on the cheek.

"Grab a sweater," he advised. "It's cold out there."

"It's hanging on the banister," she told him. "But thanks."

He led her outside where Lisa found it *was* cold, a cold she wasn't expecting. Martin helped her into the car and sped off down the road.

Hours later they returned home. They'd tried something different for both dinner and dessert and had managed to almost finish the wine. Martin had led her to the dance floor where they had almost made love. They continued teasing each other all the way home and found themselves undressing each other on the way upstairs.

It wasn't long before they were on the bed and Martin was passionately making love to her.

"You looked absolutely delectable tonight," he told her.

"You didn't look so bad yourself," she replied.

They hurried and climaxed together making it worthwhile and both fell asleep quickly.

CHAPTER 13

Lisa woke early the next morning. She just couldn't sleep any longer and she snuck downstairs where she made herself a cup of tea and disappeared into the dining room. She was sure there had to be something more so she opened a few of the shoeboxes expecting to find shoes. Most of them did contain shoes and she closed them and set them aside. She was surprised, when she opened the last one, to find a stack of papers and other things tucked inside.

She pulled them out one by one and realized she'd hit the jackpot. Inside was a wallet that still contained identification and it was then that she found out she was correct about the initials *S-L*, they stood for *Sophia Ledoux*. She found a birth certificate dating back to the late 1800's as well as a few other superfluous items that were no longer even available. There were also some pictures inside of an infant and she realized that Martin had been dreaming about this baby.

Further along there was a birth announcement for a baby girl with a few well wishes cards and at the very bottom of the box was a death certificate, folded in half and when Lisa opened it, a yellowed obituary fell out. She read both and realized that the baby was only about six months old when Sophia had died.

"That's horrible," she said out loud as she began putting everything back into the box.

"What is?" Martin asked startling her.

Lisa almost jumped out of her chair. "Don't do that! I'm reading about a dead woman who's obviously haunting us and you scare me like that."

"I'm sorry," Martin said and kneeled before her. "I didn't mean to," he said with a pout on his lips. He reached up and kissed her. "I just want to say *good morning.*"

Lisa smiled and melted with the kiss. She knew he'd had no intentions of scaring her, she was just so deep in thought... her mind stopped as Martin's kisses had continued to her neck and he was now kissing her thighs. He pulled her forward slightly on the chair and parted her bathrobe. She looked down and met his eyes before he slid a tongue across the inside of her thigh. She reached down and ran her fingers through his hair rhythmically just before she was about to climax, and then she cried out.

Martin smiled at being able to bring her such pleasure and he rose on his knees to join her. He slid inside her and could still feel the rhythmic contractions.

It didn't take him long to reach his own climax and he held tight to her.

They ate breakfast while Lisa told Martin everything she'd found in the box. "I want to go to the library today and go through all the old newspapers. Maybe I can find something else," she told him.

"Did the obituary give any hints?" Martin asked.

"I didn't get a chance to read it, that's when you came in and scared me half to death," she admitted.

"Then why don't you read it first."

They cleaned up after their breakfast and she went back to the dining room to look at the obituary while Martin went upstairs to shower.

She joined him moments later, sliding her hands over his wet chest. "It didn't say much. Commented about an accidental death at home and asked for donations to their church."

Martin again nodded. "I'll come with you if you want," he told her.

Lisa nodded. She thought two heads working on this would be better and told him so.

"And here I thought we could go make out between the stacks," he said and teased her ear with his tongue.

"Always an ulterior motive," she replied as she sucked in a sharp breath as his tongue dipped at a very sensitive spot at her collar bone. "Make love to me now Martin," she pled.

"My pleasure," he replied and boosted her up against the wall of the shower and pressed himself inside her.

They finished their lovemaking in bed before they dressed and left for town.

"We do need to get groceries while we're in town," he advised.

Lisa nodded as Martin pulled into a small parking lot outside an even smaller building.

"Here we are," he said.

"This is it?" she asked wondering how many books a building this size could hold.

"This *is* it, what did you expect?" he asked.

"I thought it might be larger than a phone booth," she said.

Martin couldn't hold in his laughter. "Well we don't have a lot of people, so we don't have a huge library."

"Will it have newspaper archives?" she asked.

"Yes, it *does* have the archives as a matter of fact, I think they're in that little slot people put quarters in."

Lisa gave him a playful swat. "You're nothing but trouble," she told him.

He laughed at her again and leaned over and gave her a kiss. "Let's go."

They got out of the car and went inside. The first floor was entirely fiction and a sign pointing to the upstairs indicated it was the kids' floor.

"We're going this way," Martin said pulling her towards the stairs.

"But that's the kids' floor," she said but was surprised when he pulled her downstairs instead.

"Nope, this way," he told her.

Downstairs was an entirely different story. It was huge and seemed to span beneath the parking lot as well.

They started through some of the old newspapers, which they knew would be on microfilm, and had to examine the directory before they could determine approximately where it was they needed to start.

"I think I found something," Martin said.

Lisa left her machine and walked over behind Martin. She automatically put her hands on his shoulders and leaned down close to him. It felt wonderful to be able to do this and she added a peck on his cheek before she looked at what he'd found.

Woman Reported Missing, Leaves Infant Child

A Goderich woman has been reported missing for forty-eight hours. Her husband states she's been feeling unwell since the birth of her baby and hopes she just went away for a bit of a break.

Police have searched the entire area, interviewed family and friends and have come up with nothing at this point.

If you have any information, please contact police.

"It's definitely a start," Lisa said after she'd read it. "At least we have a smaller time frame now."

Martin nodded. He felt he knew what was going to happen, where it was all going to go from here.

Lisa decided to check a few of the papers in the week following the initial article and it was quite some time before she called to Martin she had found something more.

Martin went to her and set his hands on her shoulders and began reading what she had found.

Missing Woman Found

A Goderich woman, who was reported missing three days ago, has been found. Her body washed up on the beach in Bayfield. Police are only revealing she drowned and are trying to re-create what happened. They are suspecting foul play but are not certain at this time, they may be ruling this out fairly early in the investigation.

"Guess that explains a little more," Lisa said quietly as Martin pressed the 'print' button to make a copy.

Lisa went back to her machine, after retrieving her printout, and this time switched to the internet and using a search engine typed in 'Sophia Ledoux'.

An entire listing came up but some referenced the newspaper. "Argh," she groaned.

"What's wrong?" Martin asked looking over at her.

"You would think I would have thought to run a search on the internet first," she said.

"Why, did you find something more?" he asked. He too was a little perturbed as he never thought of that either.

Lisa clicked on one of the most detailed options and it took her to an entire page. Scanning it, she began to read chunks out loud to Martin.

"Sophia Ledoux... 24 when she died... lived in manor house on Lake Huron... baby born in March of 1920... died in September... drowned in the lake... now feel it was one of the first known cases of postpartum depression and she was never treated..." Lisa trailed off.

Martin watched her face as she figured it all out.

"She committed suicide by going out into the lake at night with heavy winds creating an undertoe that would certainly pull her under. All because of postpartum depression," she said. "That's so sad. No wonder she haunts the place."

Martin smiled. "I don't think the little we've seen classifies as a haunting, I just think she wanted us to know the truth."

Lisa shrugged. She hit 'print' to make a copy of this as well and they left the library just the way they'd found it.

It wasn't until they got to the car that Martin leaned over and kissed her while he slid his hand over hers. "We didn't make out in the stacks," he told her.

Lisa laughed. It was just what she needed after all she'd discovered. "We could go back inside," she replied.

Martin made for the door handle and they both burst into laughter. "Let's go get some food," he said and started the car.

Grocery shopping always seemed quite the chore to Lisa but Martin somehow made it fun and they left there in quite a happy mood.

When they arrived back at the house, they managed to get everything inside in one trip and Lisa helped Martin unpack the bags while they talked about what had happened.

"I just can't believe that it was just postpartum depression," Lisa said. "There are so many things that can be done for that today," she added.

"But that was over 80 years ago, Lisa, they didn't have the medical advances we have now," he reminded her.

"I know, I forget sometimes, but you would think they would have figured it out," she replied.

"But she didn't even seek medical attention, probably like the millions of other depression sufferers who never go to the doctor because they think it will pass."

Lisa shrugged uncertain of what else she could say. She took the pages they'd printed and set them in the dining room with all the other things in there. *What else are you trying to tell us?* Lisa wondered. Then she wondered about what had happened to the baby.

Martin found Lisa in the dining room. "What's up?" he asked.

"Just wondering whatever happened to the baby," she replied.

Martin shrugged. "Probably ended up being raised by her dad," he speculated.

Lisa made a mental note to go back to the website and see if there was more there than what she had read at the library.

Martin made lunch while Lisa went upstairs to freshen up. She sat in the chair by the window and just watched the waves, so far away from here. It was hard to believe that it was cold enough outside to no longer be able to swim. Her mind then turned to her own life and the turmoil it was in. She didn't want to leave here, it was certainly beautiful, and she was no longer certain she even wanted to return to the financial world anymore. She was at a point in her life where she was wondering if she had a different calling, she was at the fork in the road so to speak, and she had to make the choice. She knew she'd be walking down the path with a new husband and then she wondered if there was a baby at the end of one of the laneways.

"What are you thinking about?" Martin asked as he walked into the room. "You look awfully serious."

"Just thinking about the fork in the road and the decisions I have to make so I can choose to move down one path," she replied.

"Like what?" he asked.

"Like whether I want to return to the world of finance or pursue other avenues. Of course, and there's no pressure at all, knowing whether there is a baby in my future would be a help as well."

Martin met her gaze. "I'm not sure," he said slowly. "I never gave that much thought, I was just enjoying you so much..." he trailed off. "I'm sorry."

Lisa looked at him. "I told you there was no pressure," she reminded him again. "I just realized too that it was something we need to discuss more."

Martin began thinking too. His one concern was if he'd be able to father a child at his age. He was also concerned about what would happen in the event of his death. "I think we do need to talk about this more," he told her. "But right now, lunch is served in the kitchen."

He held a hand out to her and led her downstairs where they ate in almost complete silence.

"I need to use the internet," Lisa said as she got up and left the room leaving Martin watching after her.

He gave her a quick nod and started clearing the dishes. She was right to ask about a baby. She wasn't even 30 after all. He wanted to give her the family she would someday be looking for.

When he finished cleaning up the kitchen, he put on a heavy jacket and went out the back door. He didn't say anything to her, he just wanted to think. He headed for the beach and just started walking. He first counted how old he might live to be and then determined how old a child might be when it was time for him to leave. He realized he might make it to see a high school graduation and thought that might just be worth it. He started walking back toward the house and couldn't wait to tell Lisa.

Lisa sat at the computer checking her email. Gerry had finally replied and told her he was happy for her but he really needed her at the branch so he would appreciate knowing as soon as possible and he would certainly put in a good word for her at the Goderich branch if she chose to transfer.

Before that, she'd gone back to the site about Sophia Ledoux and read that the father had taken the baby and moved away, neither to be heard from again. She wondered if that was why Sophia was restless, she was still looking for her baby.

"Hey," Martin said on his return. He slid his hands over her shoulders.

"You're cold, where have you been?" she asked.

"I took a walk," he told her. "I had some of my own thinking to do."

She nodded. "Well, I'm still working on it," she told him. "But I did find out that the father of Sophia's baby took the baby and left. Nobody's heard from them since."

Martin sank down on his knees in front of her. "Maybe we'll have to look into that for her," he said. He took both her hands in his own. "Lisa, I had to think about something and do a little math," he told her with a chuckle. "But I would love to have children with you."

"Really?" she asked.

"Yes, really," he replied.

They went upstairs and slid into bed where they spent the rest of the afternoon in bed, making love and talking quietly.

They discussed getting married the following Valentine's Day which didn't leave a lot of time for planning but since they'd already decided to have the reception at the house, that part was planned and out of the way and maybe they didn't need to get married in the backyard at sunset anyway.

"Let's think about it for a day or two," Martin said. "We'll decide then what we're going to do."

Lisa nodded in agreement and kissed him, which started their lovemaking all over again.

"I think I should make us some dinner," Martin said an hour later. "This has been a long day, I'm tired, how are you feeling?"

"I'm thrilled about what we found out and happy we want to try and have a baby," she replied. "But yeah, I'm feeling a little tired too."

Martin decided just to make some homemade soup and Lisa helped with what she could. They sat down in the dining room and made a list of as much information they could find in the limited documents they had. Lisa hadn't come across anything concrete on the website about the family background so she didn't know where else to start.

They ate in front of a fire in the den that evening telling stories about their childhoods. Martin had been an only child and regretted not having siblings. His father had become ill when he was a teenager which left his mom to raise him. She did her best but had to work a lot and he was left to finish the job on his own. He had gone into the world of finance himself at a young age since that's what was flourishing at the time. He knew the stresses of it all and he understood that Lisa may want to get out of it. Lisa had her two siblings that had driven her nuts over the course of her childhood. She hated that her parents were never able to afford for her to pursue interests and activities and had to grow up fast in order to provide childcare for them. She had gone to university but wasn't certain upon graduation what she really wanted to do so she continued on with what had been a part time job for her through college and trained to become what she was today.

After they had finished eating and cleared away the dishes, Martin pulled her onto the floor where they cuddled and continued chatting. Lisa shared with him that she'd always wanted to learn ballroom dance and he admitted that he'd always wanted to go for a balloon ride. Lisa shuddered at the thought.

"What? I think it would be beautiful," he said defending what he wanted to do.

"It's not that I disagree, however, I believe it's quite cold up there and I'm concerned about crashing," she said.

"Oh, I never thought of that, but I guess taking a balloon ride over the lake would be extra dangerous wouldn't it?"

Lisa nodded but if he was willing to learn a few extra dance steps with her, she was willing to scream her way through a balloon ride.

Martin dragged Lisa off to bed with little effort and vowed the next night he would draw a hot bath for her and break open a bottle of wine. He even thought he'd set out some candles. Then he realized he would do his best to make that a surprise.

They made love and he wrapped her into his arms and waited quietly before she went to sleep before he relaxed and went to sleep.

CHAPTER 14

Sunday morning dawned bright and warm and Martin didn't let go of his plan but he did drag her out of bed and told her to get dressed as he wanted to take her to church.

Lisa didn't argue as she really did want to go to church this morning. She hated missing as she liked to be reminded of God's love as sometimes it was the only thing that kept her going in a week. She showered and dressed while Martin made breakfast and they ate together looking out over the lake before Martin got up and went to shower.

Lisa sat staring at the lake, waves washing up on shore relentlessly, in their own pattern at their own rhythm. She wondered how God had created something so wonderful that could sort of take care of itself. She also wanted to know how her own life could turn into that and she closed her eyes. *God, how can I calm down and how can I make things right for my life? What do You expect from me and what decisions do you want me to make? I'm kind of on a bit of a time schedule here. I'm so thankful for the surprises you have given me on this trip and I thank you for showing me the way to love. I just want to do the right thing and I truly need your guidance.*

She whispered "Amen" before she gave her eyelids a quick squeeze for no reason whatsoever and opened them to look back upon the lake almost glowing in the sunlight. She looked down and smoothed her skirt, picking a piece of lint off of it.

"What are you thinking about?" Martin asked as he came out of the bathroom wrapped in a towel.

"Just thinking," she said. "Saying a prayer."

Martin nodded. He thought he understood even though he wasn't sure he did fully. He dressed as he watched her closely and wondered what it was she was thinking.

They left shortly after that and Martin introduced her to almost everyone at the church. They all wanted to know who she was and when they found out she was his fiancée, they became very animated.

Lisa didn't know what to make of everyone. She knew that people in small towns tended to be this way, extra friendly, but she certainly wasn't used to it. She greeted them graciously and accepted their congratulations' in the same way.

She held Martin's hand through the service which was very similar to that of her own church at home. It made her feel a lot better and the minister seemed like a great guy so she gave Martin's hand a squeeze and listened intently to the sermon. Part way through she had to reach up and wipe away a tear as it seemed that he was speaking only to her. She kept silently saying *thank you* to God and listened so intently she started squeezing Martin's hand.

"You okay?" he leaned over and asked.

She could only nod and wipe away more tears as she began to see everything coming into focus.

She had worked hard in university but in the end had only gotten a Bachelor of Arts because she wasn't sure what she had wanted to major in. She had done some psychology courses as well as political science and had actually majored in English as she had enjoyed all of the writing courses. It was then that she realized she was to start writing a book. *And what a wonderful place to do it,* she thought. The lake, the house, the entire atmosphere and she would take any part-time position open at the Goderich branch in order to keep paying the bills. That wasn't exactly what she was thinking and the idea of possibly working at one of the little stores downtown suddenly started to appeal to her more and she wondered about the bookstore.

The service came to a close shortly after the sermon ended and the offering had been collected.

"So what's up?" Martin asked as he grabbed her hand and led her down the aisle.

"Everything just got a lot clearer," she told him. She was still trying to fathom the thoughts herself so was having some difficulties trying to put it into words at the moment.

"Are you going to share?" he asked leaning close to her ear.

"I am but do you mind if I take a bit of walk by myself first?" she asked. She saw the odd look on his face and added "I just need to collect my thoughts and get things on paper," she explained.

Martin nodded. He had a feeling this was a good thing but then he thought maybe he was just deluding himself.

They shook hands with the minister before Martin led her out to the car and helped her in.

"I'm going to make some lunch, why don't you go get changed," Martin suggested.

Lisa nodded and went upstairs where she changed and pulled out a pad of paper and a pen. She began scribbling, as her mind was racing, down everything she'd thought of in church; the idea about the job and the idea of writing a book. It still sounded wonderful to her, she just needed to head down to the beach to work up the courage to tell certain people and start following through with her plans. She also realized she should take a trip into town so she could see if the bookstore was even looking for help before she completely walked away from the bank. If they weren't hiring now, maybe she could stay at the branch for a while.

"Hey, how are you making out?" Martin asked quietly as he entered the room.

"I'm doing just fine, how's lunch coming along?" she asked as she stood and walked over to him. He still had his tie on and she was getting quite turned on at the idea of removing it. She reached up and slowly began to untie it.

Martin moaned quietly and let her slowly remove his tie and then proceed to unbuttoning his shirt. He sucked in a breath at her touch when she slid her hands inside and splayed them across his flesh. He felt himself becoming very aroused and he finally leaned down and captured her mouth with his own. His tongue surged into her mouth and before they were both aware of what was happening, he had led her to the bed and they were both naked and making love to each other.

"Oh God Lisa, I love you so much," Martin called out to her.

"I love you too, darling," Lisa called back.

After, they lay sated next to each other and Martin finally told her lunch should be ready, if not burnt.

Lisa giggled at how out of control things had gotten and when she explained it to Martin, he laughed too.

They only slid into robes to eat and Lisa helped him tidy up the kitchen before she retreated to the bedroom to get dressed again and get ready to take her walk. The weather had taken a change for the better and was supposed to hit 20 degrees. When she checked the outdoor thermometer it was already 21 so she dressed only in a t-shirt.

"I'll be back soon," she told him as she kissed him on the cheek and disappeared out the door. Since church she felt a lot lighter than she had in a while and she realized how right her thoughts and ideas were. She looked to the skies when she reached the bottom of the stairs and said a prayer asking that she be given guidance if the decisions she was making weren't the right ones.

Tears came to her eyes as she began walking. There was only a light breeze coming off the lake and she thought of everything she would be leaving behind but of all the new things she would be discovering. The idea that Martin wanted to have a baby with her, the thought of writing a book and working in a bookstore spending time with what she loved. The drive back home was only an hour and a quarter away so why shouldn't she make the move. It would be truly amazing and getting her family to come visit now and again would be wonderful. True vacations, what a thought. She rubbed her stomach as she wasn't feeling well and wondered what it was that she'd had again. She realized it wasn't anything she should react to and figured that perhaps it was all the stress she'd been carrying around. She face the water and watched it reflecting the sunshine above. She revelled in the glory of it all. How absolutely wonderful it all was. She knew she had to go back to the house and talk to Martin. She didn't have a choice. She needed to let him know what she was thinking and then sit down and make a list of how she was going to proceed. Her time was running out to let Gerry know she wouldn't be back and she felt bad that he would miss her and needed her but then she realized that it was seriously wearing her down and there was nothing that was really going to make her feel better. She was run off her feet at her job and the demand of customers was becoming too great to bear anymore. They wanted everything she couldn't guarantee and then got angry with her when their investments took a loss and she spent more time reassuring them that long term investments would do that, it was to be expected and there was nothing she could do and that they shouldn't worry. She felt the frustrations and stress from it all starting to well up inside her and she knew she was making the right decisions.

She walked slowly up the stairs and sat down in one of the chairs at the top and just looked out over the lake.

Martin saw her from the kitchen window and couldn't help but go out to her. He approached her slowly as he didn't want to startle her. "Hi."

"Hey, why don't you sit down?" she asked. "It's a beautiful day," she said.

Martin smiled and took the seat next to her. He reached for her hand and rubbed her thumb with his own.

"I've had to make some decisions and the sermon this morning seemed to be speaking solely to me. It was incredible and I couldn't help but see things start to fall into place." She proceeded to tell him what she had thought about and that her next step was to make a list of everything she needed to do at this point, including getting to the bookstore to see if they needed help.

Martin nodded and made all the right noises at all the right places and then asked her if she was sure.

Lisa nodded. "I'm still going to have to get used to the idea, but yeah, I'm sure," she assured him.

They sat there quietly for what seemed like forever, Lisa leaning back on Martin as they just watched the lake, how peaceful it was after the last few days of stormier weather and could only wonder what their future would bring and being thankful for what they had already received.

CHAPTER 15

Lisa went back upstairs when they went inside and Martin made a pot of tea.

She carried her pad downstairs and sat at the computer. She knew she couldn't let Gerry know yet because she needed to find out a few things here.

When she was finished as far as she could go until she did her further research, she ran a search again on Sophia Ledoux and when she realized she hadn't finished looking through all of Sophia's things, she went to the dining room, passing through the kitchen.

"Steeping the tea right now," he said.

"That's great, I'll be right back," she said. She ducked into the dining room and began rummaging through the papers they hadn't figured were all that important and finally came across a folded, yellow piece of paper and she carefully unfolded it, afraid it would rip and fall apart.

It was in fact the marriage certificate and she could barely make out the names as the ink had faded so badly. She moved into the light and had to move it around a bit before she finally made out the name Isaac. She assumed the last name would be the same and she carried the piece of paper with her. She was surprised to discover that Sophia had either kept her own last name *Ledoux*, or just hadn't had the opportunity to change it and she wondered why that was as every woman changed her name when she got married in those days. *Isaac Shantz* was the name on the marriage license and she entered that name into the search engine. Not much came up on him so again she was at a loss. She wondered if anyone around town would know what had happened to the father and the baby.

"Here's your tea," Martin said setting a cup beside the computer. "What have you found out?" he asked.

She shrugged. "Not much actually. I can make out the name *Isaac Shantz* on the marriage license but he wasn't very famous as there's not a lot online about the man." She removed her fingers from the keyboard and took a sip of the tea.

"Would you like a snack?" Martin asked.

Lisa nodded but had already turned her attention back to the computer. After Martin left the room, she stood and went to the dining room again where she looked through the things since she hadn't found a lot on the baby either. She came across an envelope that had never been opened and very carefully slid her finger under the flap and opened it. She removed what was inside and found it was the birth certificate for Anna Sophia Shantz. It stated she was born March 20th, 1920.

She went back to the computer where she typed in that name and got far more results than she'd hoped for. Martin had brought in some cookies and cheese on a plate and she casually reached and helped herself without even looking. Then she groaned with frustration.

"What's wrong?" Martin asked looking up from the magazine article he was reading.

"I found the name of the baby and there's several thousand results that came up when I entered it in. Seems

Anna Shantz is a well-known writer and there's no way I can determine if it's the same one except that she still lives in the area."

"Call her or pay her a visit, does it say where she lives?"

"She's at a nursing home in town, maybe we could pay her a visit."

"We can try that sometime this week," Martin said, his mind distracted by his reading.

Lisa nodded and turned her attention back to what she was reading. She couldn't believe how many books this woman had written.

She gave up and shut the computer down before she carried her tea over to Martin and after setting it down on the coffee table, she lay down, putting her head in his lap and looking up at him.

Martin couldn't resist any longer and he set down his magazine. He stroked her hair and watched as her eyes fluttered closed, then open again. "Tired?" he asked.

She nodded. "A little."

They discussed a few scenarios about what had possibly gone on over 80 years ago and couldn't come up with anything concrete.

Lisa started to formulate a plan in her mind and smiled.

"What are you smiling about?" he asked her.

"I'm thinking I'll use the excuse of buying one of Anna's books to go to the bookstore, then I'll talk to the owner about a job."

"Sounds like the start of a plan," Martin replied. "Hey, when do you think you'll move your things?" he asked.

Lisa's eyes opened wide. "I, I don't know," she replied. "I hadn't actually thought about it," she admitted.

"I didn't think you had," he said. "But you're still paying rent and probably don't need that extra expense," he reminded her.

"You're right and if I give notice before the end of this month, I will only have to pay one more month," she said working it out as she spoke.

Martin lifted her head. "I'm going to go put that roast in the oven," he told her as he helped her sit up so he could get out from under her.

Lisa nodded and after he left the room, despite the fact she had so much on her mind, her eyes still fluttered closed and stayed that way.

Martin walked back in the room and didn't realize at first that she was asleep but as he moved toward her, he realized that her breathing was very shallow and that she had to be sleeping. He pulled the blanket off the back of the armchair and covered her up. Just then the phone rang and he went to the kitchen to answer it.

He forgot that he'd put the message on about them being closed until spring, but since it was also his personal line, he didn't have a choice but to answer.

"Hello?" he said into the phone as he began pulling potatoes from the pantry. He listened intently as the person on the other end asked if there was any way he had a room available over Christmas and when he was finally able to get a word in edgewise he informed them that no, he did not. They seemed disappointed and tried very hard to deter the answer but he told them that unfortunately he was going to be out of town and had nobody to cover for him at the house.

He shook his head in frustration when he hung up the phone and went on to peel the potatoes. When all was done, he sat at the breakfast bar and reflected on the last week. How the love of his life had walked into his B&B and he hadn't known she was out there. How did he ever get so lucky? What was he going to pay in return? He shrugged his shoulder and pulled over a piece of paper. He made a list of ideas for their wedding. He knew that once Lisa got settled she'd get right into the plans but he thought that depending on what date they chose, he would need to made a few bookings almost right away. He wasn't certain if she really liked his idea of Valentine's Day as he knew she had wanted to get married out back with the sun setting in the background when they'd first discussed it. He wrote that down as well before he set it aside and hurried to remove the lid from the potato pot before it boiled over.

He wasn't sure what it was exactly that brought tears to his eyes but something made him feel extremely emotional about all that was going on in his life.

When all was under control in the kitchen, he went back to check in on Lisa who was still sleeping soundly but had partly kicked the blanket off so he fixed it for her, turned on the lamp over the armchair and grabbed his magazine and began reading again.

Lisa moaned softly then her eyes fluttered open.

"Hey beautiful, have a good sleep?" Martin asked looking over the top of a book he had switched to after he'd read all the articles he was interested in.

She nodded and yawned. "Did you cover me up?" she asked.

Martin raised an eyebrow.

Lisa chuckled. "Of course you did right?" she asked.

Martin chuckled then too. "I could have said it was a new guest that had signed in then saw you and covered you up."

Lisa shook her head. "Okay, okay, I get it."

"Dinner's almost ready," he told her.

She started to sit up and realized she was a little lightheaded so she sank back down for a few moments. She was hoping Martin hadn't noticed but it was too late.

"You okay?" he asked suddenly concerned.

"Yeah, I just sat up too fast," she told him. She was sure that was the problem. She used to have that all the time.

Martin got up and said he'd be back in a second and left the room.

Lisa sat up again, this time slowly, and had no further problem. She set the blanket aside and stood slowly before she went upstairs to the bathroom. She freshened up a little and went back downstairs to help Martin move all of Sophia's things to the other end of the dining room table and put some back in the trunk so they could set the table for dinner.

Martin dimmed the lights, lit the candles and turned on a CD of piano music for them to enjoy while they ate.

"Oh, nice," Lisa complimented him.

"Thank you my dear, it's for you."

He brought food in and they sat down to eat. "Did you have a good sleep?" he asked again.

"I did. I can't believe I was that tired though," she replied.

"I think you've had an emotional day," he reminded her.

She nodded thinking back to her time in church that morning and then her walk on the beach. She nodded again.

They ate quietly, each lost in thought and it wasn't until Lisa pushed her plate away and took a gulp of her wine that either spoke. "So what's for dessert?" she asked.

Martin rose from his chair and knelt between her knees. He slid a hand up her leg, over her stomach and rested it on her breast.

"Mmmm," she moaned. "I like it so far."

He slid his hands under her sweater and undid her bra before he cupped both of her breasts. He slid the sweater up and suckled at each breast for what felt like an eternity to Lisa who pressed her fingers into his scalp. She squirmed in her chair and felt his tongue licking her nipple which sent her to ecstasy levels. "Oh God Martin, make love to me," she told him.

He didn't need to hear anymore and he took her hand and led her upstairs where he did just that until they were both sated.

Martin put his arms around Lisa and they fell asleep that way.

CHAPTER 16

Lisa woke hours later to find darkness surrounded the house. She slid out of bed as she really had to pee and then proceeded to move about quietly closing the blinds. She realized there was light coming from downstairs and she went down to find the dining room the way they'd left it. She had napped before dinner and had fallen asleep so early that she had quite a bit of energy so she cleared the table and tidied up the dining room. She was grateful that the candles had just burned out and hadn't burned the house down and she made a mental note to at least reprimand Martin about that in the morning. She double checked the dining room and noticed that the small silver carriage was almost glowing in the darkness and she walked over to it and picked it up. She had intense feelings that came to her and she was sure there was more to the story than she'd first thought. She thought she'd go back online in the morning and see about finding more of a background on Anna at the very least since she'd pretty well exhausted all she could about Sophia.

She climbed back upstairs and slid back into bed beside Martin who hadn't moved and felt better that everything in the house was secure. She drifted back off to sleep.

Martin woke the next morning and looked down at his fiancée, so beautiful in the little bit of light that crept through the cracks in the blinds. His thoughts turned to the night before and he instantly felt aroused. *Oh God, this is never going to stop is it?* He thought. His hands began to roam her body. Her flesh so warm, her breathing shallow and slow. His lips pressed against her neck and he began caressing her.

Lisa woke to Martin's lips on her neck and she moaned with pleasure again when she realized he was caressing her. It didn't take long for her to climax because she was relaxed from sleeping. "Make love to me," she whispered in the semi-darkness.

Martin did just that and held her. "I need breakfast," Martin said when he'd caught his breath.

He got out of bed and went downstairs while Lisa stretched out and smiled. There was lots she wanted to do today and she knew she had to get out of bed to get it done. First she would find out whether she had a job here in town or if she was doomed to going back to the financial world for a while longer. She stretched one last time and slid out of bed. She yawned and then went to the bathroom before she went downstairs.

"Morning sleepyhead," Martin said as she walked into the kitchen wearing only her bathrobe.

"Morning, but who are you calling sleepyhead?" she asked. It was the first time she'd actually looked at the clock and was surprised it was 9:45.

"You took longer to get out of bed," he replied innocently.

"Is that so?" she asked. "You'd still be up there if it wasn't for your feeding schedule," she teased.

"Tell me you weren't starving."

"I admit I was, I am," she agreed. "We had quite the dessert last night."

Martin nodded in full agreement. "We certainly did." He gave her a kiss and served breakfast.

As they ate, they talked about what they were going to do for the day.

"Since it's been so nice lately, I'm afraid I'm going to have to cut the grass again," Martin told her.

"I really need to get into town if I'm going to get anything done," she said.

"Then that's when I'll cut the grass," he replied.

They cleared away the few breakfast dishes and went to shower. Despite having other ideas, they ended up making love in the shower and then helped each other dry off.

Lisa dressed in a warm sweater and jeans for her jaunt into town but first she turned on the computer and checked the bank's website, specifically the job postings and noticed a new one that had been posted that morning for part time at the Goderich branch. She had a feeling she would discover that the bookstore was in fact *not* looking for help but for some reason the posted position still gave her hope and something to look forward to. Part time was still better than full time at this point. It would still give her the opportunity to write her book. She checked her email and found a note from Gerry telling her there was an opening and that he had already forwarded a recommendation. He was truly sorry she was leaving, or rather not returning, and he knew that the new branch would be very lucky to have her on staff.

Lisa was floored. She couldn't believe that, without her permission, her boss had gone ahead and made a recommendation for her for a job she wasn't even certain she wanted to take.

"What's up?" Martin asked as he entered the room and saw the look on her face.

"Gerry made a recommendation to the branch up here, they just posted a job this morning," she explained.

"Wow," he said quietly. "But..." he trailed off.

"Yeah, I wasn't even sure I wanted something like that," she affirmed. "But now I'll have to get in there with an application I suppose."

"I guess the sooner the better then," Martin agreed. He knew it wasn't really what she wanted and he was afraid to venture any further into the conversation. "Is it full time?" he asked cautiously.

She shook her head. "No, it's only part time, which would be okay I guess. I'm assuming it's an omen and how can I deny that?" she asked.

Martin shrugged. He'd never met someone so intuitively connected to things. Seeing things as omens rather than just life happening. She tried so hard to be positive all the time, looking inside for answers rather than taking what came at her. This time he had to agree with her, it was luck, or fate or whatever she believed in because how else would something like this have happened? "Why don't you do that while you go to the bookstore?" he said. "Go in and talk to them."

Lisa nodded. She'd have to change her clothes to something a little more appropriate for a possible interview. She gave up at the computer and stood.

Martin gave her a hug. "No matter what happens," he said.

She smiled up at him. He didn't care either way what she did, as long as it made her happy and knowing that made her happy. "I love you."

"I love you too, now go," he told her giving her a gentle swat on the backside.

She ran up the stairs and into the bedroom grateful she'd brought dress slacks along as well as a pair of loafers. The sweater she'd put on would be fine and she finished changing quickly. She didn't have a resume though so she hoped that just letting them know she was interested in the position would be good enough until she could get her resume retrieved from her email and printed off.

"I'm off," she called out to Martin. She couldn't find him so she went out the back and saw him just coming out of the shed. "I'm leaving," she called again.

He gave a wave and blew her a kiss. "Good luck sweetheart and see you soon."

She blew a kiss back at him and went out to her car hoping it would start after all this time. It turned over with no problem and aside from the brakes being a little soft, it ran just fine and she headed towards town. It felt good to be off on her own and she felt like taking the drive back home, but then she realized that this was her home in so many ways. She didn't miss the hustle and bustle of the city at all. She reached downtown quickly and easily and worked her way around the square until she found a parking spot outside the bookstore. She smiled before she got out of the car and made her way inside.

"Hi there," the owner said from behind the counter. "Can I help you?" she asked.

"My name is Lisa Davies and aside from needing something to read, I also wanted to know if you were looking for any help," she said.

The owner looked at her sceptically. "My name is Sheryl Shantz and I own the place. I usually run it myself though and tend to just need help around the holidays. Are you new here?" she asked.

Lisa nodded a little disappointed to say the least. "I'm marrying Martin Hurst," she said quietly.

"Our best eligible bachelor?" Sheryl asked.

Lisa nodded. "I guess," she said unaware of his 'status'.

"Well aren't you lucky. Anyway, have a look around and before you leave I'll get your name and number and call you if I'm in need of help around the holidays."

"Thank you Sheryl," Lisa said. "You wouldn't happen to be related to Anna Sophia Shantz would you?" she asked, skeptical herself that there was a connection.

Sheryl's eyes grew wide. "How, why, uh, did you think to ask that?" Sheryl asked completely flustered.

"Let's just say we've had some, um, *communication* out at the house," Lisa replied.

"Really?" Sheryl asked. "I'd always heard that place was haunted, I just never believed it."

"Why is that? Because it's your family's?" Lisa asked.

Sheryl nodded then stopped. "No, well, it's complicated," she began. "There were always so many rumours. My grandmother, Anna, never knew anything about them," Sheryl went on. She took a deep breath and went on. "Then she learned about everything on her father's deathbed. It wasn't a pretty story in the end."

"I was going to go visit Anna," Lisa told her. "I was hoping perhaps I could finally, after all these years, put her mother's soul to rest."

Sheryl looked at her with raised eyebrows. "You really think that sort of thing works?" she asked doubtfully.

"I truly believe it," Lisa told her confidently.

"I could tell you what you want to know," Sheryl said quietly.

"You could but do you want to?" Lisa asked. "I'm getting the feeling it ended more the way that I suspected than the way the newspapers told it."

"You're right," Sheryl said nodding.

"Then tell me and I promise I won't bother your grandmother unless it's to tell her what's happened in person."

Sheryl sucked in a deep breath and closed her eyes. Then she opened them. "Could we do lunch?" she asked.

"Yeah," Lisa replied surprised.

"Do you have any other errands to run? I can close the store for an hour at noon," she told her.

Lisa nodded. "I do actually. I need to go to the bank."

Sheryl told her to go and come back at noon and they could go for lunch.

Lisa left the store feeling a bit frazzled. She wasn't sure she liked Sheryl, she certainly had a chip on her shoulder. What about Lisa was never sure she'd ever know but Lisa was more sure the posting this morning was a blessing in disguise. She crossed the square and entered the branch and before she could read nameplates on office doors her hand was being shook by a man she figured to be the branch manager.

"Lisa Davies?" he asked.

Lisa nodded. "How on earth did you know?" she asked, more surprised than she was when Martin had proposed to her.

"Gerry is an old friend of mine and along with an absolutely glowing recommendation with a hidden threat or two buried in there, he also happened to send along your picture. I've been waiting for you all morning, come into my office, sit down, can I get you a coffee?" he asked.

Lisa wondered if the man ever took a breath and she let him lead her through a doorway that said Peter Mason on the nameplate. "I'd love a cup thank you," she replied.

"Have a seat, I'll bring in coffee," Peter said and left the office.

Whoa, what the hell was that? She asked herself and gave her head a little shake.

Peter was back within seconds and set a steaming mug in front of her.

"Thank you Mr..." she was cut off before she could finish.

"It's Pete, nothing more and certainly nothing as formal as *mister*," he said.

She was again taken aback by his friendliness and realized that all of this must come from the small town atmosphere. She nodded and began to apologize but Pete only held up a hand to stop her.

"Let's get down to why you're here," he began. "I've read Gerry's letter, repeatedly and I've checked up on you in the database. There is no reason why I shouldn't hire you and there's certainly no reason why I don't want to hire you so when can you start?"

Again Lisa was shocked. This was beyond any expectations she'd had when she'd driven into town and she didn't know how to start. "Well, I'm on vacation right now," she began.

Pete looked at her and waited quietly while she went on.

Lisa didn't know how she was doing or what he was thinking. She was worried that he wasn't going to let her finish her vacation time and yet she wasn't that concerned if she was only returning part time. "I took my full four weeks and I started a week ago," she explained.

"So you wouldn't be starting until the week after Thanksgiving," he said looking at the calendar on his desk."

She nodded.

"Would you consider starting back right after Thanksgiving and taking a week at Christmas?" he asked.

Lisa hadn't thought of that and she only stared at him for a moment.

"You're staying within the company. All your seniority travels with you as does your vacation time, benefits and everything. Gerry explained you were moving here, so if you wanted time off at Christmas to go back home, you can start

early and I'll give you the time off. You've got the longest
seniority of this whole branch, except myself, so you get first
dibs."

Lisa sucked in a breath. That would work for her as
she hadn't given any thought to traveling home for Christmas
with her family and they'd probably kill her if she didn't.

They shook hands and she was hired.

"There's no need to notify Gerry, he's going to be
transferring your file, if he hasn't already started the
process."

"But how..." she trailed off.

"He's a smart man and he didn't want us to lose you. I
know it's only part time and I hope that's not a problem for
you."

Lisa shook her head. "No, it's not." She went on to
explain the circumstances that had brought her here and her
thoughts of writing as well as helping run the B&B.

"Well, you'll still keep full time status if I have a say in
it," he told her.

Lisa looked at the clock in his office and admitted she
had to get going.

He bid her farewell and told her to not be a stranger
for the remainder of her holidays but if she did get busy that
he'd see her in two weeks.

Lisa was frazzled by the time she left. She was on
overload and didn't know what to do. She took a quick walk
around the square and met Sheryl locking up the store at
noon.

"Ready for lunch?" Sheryl asked.

Lisa smiled and nodded. "Lead the way," she said.

They went to a diner just around the corner from the
store and placed their orders right away.

"So what do you want to know?" Sheryl asked cutting
to the chase.

"I just want to know what really happened to your great-grandmother," Lisa told her. "I don't want to take it to the press, I just want to know the truth."

"Well, it's not pretty, I'll tell you that right now and I don't really care if it goes to the press now or not. It would really just give Anna more publicity, more sympathy really but she heard this from her father on his death bed."

Lisa prompted her to tell the story.

Sheryl dove right in. "Apparently Anna's father had been in love with a woman named Meredith for a number of years. They didn't run in the same social classes and so they were forbidden to associate. They were the 'high school sweethearts' of today. He got drafted near the end of the war and was shipped out, so was Meredith's boyfriend at the time." She paused for the waitress to set their food down and walk away.

Lisa realized she really didn't want anyone else to know what had happened.

Sheryl took a few bites of food and commented on its tasting very good before she continued. "Anyway, he came home from war and Meredith's boyfriend did not. He didn't make it. Poor soul. I digress," she stopped again more for dramatic reasons than anything else. "So Isaac hooked up with Meredith and they met secretly as often as they could. He finally got his father to come around to the idea that Meredith was not hungry for money and didn't want the family fortune. His father, Henry, was going to force the issue of a prenuptial contract and Isaac agreed. It turned out they'd already been having sex on a very regular basis and Meredith had yet to get pregnant. Isaac wanted an heir and was determined to have one, no matter the cost. He conspired with Meredith to stage a break-up and he knew just the person he could use to have their baby."

Lisa had finished her meal at this point and was listening intently. She was surprised when she'd looked down at her plate and found it empty. "So that's all it was? A huge conspiracy?" she asked.

Sheryl took a few bites of food but nodded in response to Lisa's question. She checked the time and figured she better stop the drama and get on with it. "So they staged a break-up at the spring ball and by the end of that night he was courting Sophia. She apparently was very naïve and fell for all of it. They married almost right away and she was pregnant by June. It was in the later stages of her pregnancy that she started to put the puzzle together and realized that there may be someone else. She wasn't allowed many visitors, mostly just family and she tried her best to remain happy. Then March came around and she gave birth to a baby girl, Anna, and despite being happy about the baby, she wasn't happy about her relationship with Isaac and the midwife had made a comment at the birth, when Isaac wasn't there, that he had been seen cavorting with Meredith again.

"Sophia suffered from baby blues of course and seemed to snap out of it for a while but then in September it was confirmed he indeed was once again seeing Meredith on a very regular basis. She'd been feeling bits of what we now refer to as postpartum depression but this on top of it was too much for her. One night she got out of bed when she couldn't sleep and went downstairs and outside, down to the beach. She had to put an end to this. She wasn't in her right mind and had no concerns about her daughter.

"I guess what happened next shocked even Anna. When Sophia realized what she was doing and that the undertoe was too strong for her to fight, she began calling out for Isaac. Isaac woke to the sound of the baby crying but then heard Sophia calling to him as well. He left the baby to cry as he figured the nanny would eventually look after her, and took off outside. When he got down to the beach he could just make out her form floating in the water. He swam out to her but instead of pulling her to shore, to safety, he

held her under the water to make sure she was dead. She
wasn't and she kicked and flailed her arms to no avail and
because of her already weakened state it didn't take long. He
walked out of the lake, free for the first time, free to marry
Meredith who would raise the baby like her own. He just had
to dry his things and the nanny was in fact watching the baby.
He put on a good front and called the police at the proper
time, the whole time knowing she was already dead."

Lisa stared at Sheryl, her eyes as big as saucers. "But
why? How?" she asked. "I know why."

Sheryl shrugged her shoulders. "Up until Isaac made
this confession on his death bed, Anna thought Meredith was
her mother. She knew nothing different and nobody was
going to tell her anything more."

Lisa shook her head. "That's one of the saddest stories
I've ever heard."

Sheryl nodded in agreement.

"Do you mind if I go see Anna at some point? Just like
I said I would earlier, nothing more?" Lisa asked.

Sheryl nodded. "I don't have a problem with that.
Maybe she'll give you a signed copy of one of her books."

Lisa nodded again. "Thank you so much for telling
me. I'll see what I can do about Sophia. And maybe it will be
a matter of it going public to put her at rest."

Sheryl smiled for the first time ever. "If that's what it
will take, then you have my blessing, I think you'll have
Anna's too."

They paid their bill and each went their own way after
walking back to the store, Lisa getting in her car and Sheryl
reopening the store.

Lisa drove home with her mind on overload.
Everything that had happened in that short span of time.
The story, the job, everything. She thought for a moment she
was losing her own mind. She needed to spend the rest of
her vacation doing some serious thinking and just relaxing

after all this was resolved. She now had other things to do as well and she knew she'd spend the afternoon doing them.

CHAPTER 17

Martin met her at the door and she hadn't had much of a chance to try to work through everything from the morning on the short ten minute drive back to the house so when he asked her how things went she fumbled through trying to tell him, switching back and forth between the bank and Sheryl.

"Okay, slow down, in fact, just stop," Martin said squatting slightly and putting a hand on each shoulder and looking into her eyes. "Have you had lunch?" he asked.

"Yes, I told you I had lunch with..."

Martin cut her off. "That's all I wanted to know, now come with me." He led her upstairs, carefully removed her clothing which required a lot of control on his part, and told her to lie down on the bed. When she had done so, he went to the bathroom and got the bottle of lotion and returned. He closed the blinds down a bit to make it a more relaxing environment and turned on some music. "I'm simply going to give you a back rub and get you to relax, then you can tell me about your morning."

Lisa nodded, her face pressed into a pillow and took deep breaths as Martin's hands began to work over her back.

She suddenly felt like falling asleep and let her eyes flutter closed to stay.

"Lisa darling," Martin whispered in her ear.

"Hmmm?" was all the sound that came from her throat.

"Wake up," he told her.

Lisa turned her attention to where she was and the morning and the subsequent back rub all came back to her. "How long was I asleep?" she asked.

"An hour," he replied.

"An hour!" she said rolling over and sitting up. "Why did you let me sleep that long?"

"First, calm down," he said. "You needed it," he then said.

She was going to start all over again so Martin leaned over and kissed her. His lips pressed hard against hers and his tongue probed between her lips until she parted them and let his tongue explore her mouth.

It wasn't long before he was making love to her, her protests long forgotten.

When she climaxed, it was obvious that she had had a lot on her mind that needed ridding. He climaxed shortly after and he pulled her into his arms.

When they had both regained their composure, Martin began to ask questions. "Now, tell me what happened this morning, in order of events preferably."

Lisa laughed and took a deep breath. She replayed how Sheryl behaved and how she'd spoken to Lisa but then shared how Sheryl was Anna's great-granddaughter and actually knew what had happened all those years ago so she invited Lisa to lunch.

Martin asked some of the appropriate questions about what had happened at the bank and she brought him up to date on the whirlwind that had happened there. Then she told him she had a week's less holidays because she was going to get a week at Christmas instead. Martin wasn't upset, in fact he agreed with the manager and pointed out that Pete had been right since she probably would have regretted not being able to get home for Christmas.

Instead of proceeding to what Sheryl had told her at lunch they ended up discussing a number of things including the fact that she needed to give her superintendent notice that she was moving out, and then she needed to get her things moved out.

"Did you think that we could go down there for the long weekend and get that taken care of?" Martin asked.

Lisa shrugged. She hadn't thought of that at all but there wouldn't be any chance of that after that weekend because she'd be back at work unless she could work a couple of long shift so she could get a few days off in a row. "Yeah, we better do it then. I'll call my mom and let her know that she'll need to set two extra places for dinner."

With that much settled, Martin then asked the inevitable question. "What happened at lunch?"

Lisa took a deep breath and recounted the story Sheryl had told her about Sophia's so-called disappearance so many years ago.

Martin couldn't believe that it had been something that devious and that it had occurred 87 years ago.

"I guess people were just as devious and cruel then as they are now, the only difference is they had fewer weapons than they do now," Lisa argued.

Martin laughed knowing she was right. "So what do we do now?" he asked.

"I asked if I could still go see Anna but I think that somehow we should try to get a message to Sophia that Anna knows."

"What if we invited Anna here?"

"I guess we need to see if Anna is a believer in ghosts and if so then she'd be more open to coming here with us."

Martin nodded, "I think you're right," he said. He rolled to face her, "I think you're right about a lot of things," he said as he propped his head up on his hand and looked down at her. His other hand traced her cheek and watched as she closed her eyes and opened them again but only part way. This was a definite turn-on for him and he leaned down and kissed her.

They made love again and Martin told her to go make her calls while she remembered and slid a pair of pants on himself.

Lisa slid into her bathrobe and used the phone in the bedroom to call her superintendent to tell him she would be moving out as of the end of October and then called her mom to tell her to set two places.

"Two?" Molly asked innocently.

"Yeah mom, two, I told you I was engaged. I have to come down and settle things up at the apartment so we're going to come down for the long weekend and we'll come for dinner."

Her mom wasn't impressed at all by this piece of information and made it well known.

"Look, if you don't want Martin there, then you don't want me there. We may be getting married as soon as Valentine's Day and I want you to meet him and I want him to meet my family. If that's too difficult for you then I'll invite the rest of my family over on a day that works for everyone and we'll have a dinner of our own."

Molly gave in after that and said she'd set the extra seat.

Lisa wanted desperately to ask her mother why she just couldn't be happy for her daughter after this was what she had been bugging Lisa about for the last few years and now when it was finally happening, her mother couldn't find it in her heart to be gracious, accepting and supportive.

They hung up on amicable terms, though barely and Lisa shed only a few tears before she looked in the mirror and asked herself what she was doing. When the answer was that she was shedding tears over a heartless woman who was as two-faced as they came, she stopped crying, wiped away her tears and took a deep breath. She got dressed after that and went downstairs and out the back door. She didn't pass Martin anywhere along the way and she assumed he had found something to do. She crossed the yard and almost ran down the stairs to the beach. She stopped at the bottom and looked out over the water, taking in the view once more before she turned and started walking. There was a small bend and when she reached it, she realized that Martin was already down here and had been walking.

"What on earth are you doing down here?" Lisa asked when they had met up.

"I come down to think too sometimes," he told her.

"What brought you down here this time?" she asked, curious about what had caused him to come down to the beach and take a walk.

"I was trying to digest everything you told me in there," he said pointing at the house. "It makes me wonder how any man can treat a woman that way."

"Well don't forget that he wasn't actually in love with her," she reminded him.

"I don't think it should matter."

"I'm really glad to hear that," she said with a smile.

He smiled back at her. "I was also thinking about our wedding and that we do need to decide when we want to have it."

Lisa nodded. "I know," she replied. "I just told my mother we could get married as early as Valentine's Day," she told him. "That's really starting to grow on me you know."

"Did you mention any of that at the bank when you met with Pete this morning?" he asked.

"I did. I told him I'd just gotten engaged and that I would be getting married sometime next year and would need some time off at that point. He has no problem with that."

"Good, so should we officially set the date for Valentine's Day and get a few things booked? It's certainly going to be a busy time of year and I don't even know what day of the week that is."

"I think we should find that out but get married that day anyway."

Martin hugged her. "I love you so much."

They walked back to the house hand in hand and started making supper together. She made the salad while Martin browned some chicken breasts in a pan.

When it was all finished, Martin cut the chicken into strips and Lisa tossed it with the salad.

They sat down, smiled at one another while Martin filled two glasses with wine and made a toast to their wedding and his bride-to-be.

After they had finished eating and cleaned up the kitchen, Martin went and found a new calendar and they looked up Valentine's Day. He had built a fire so they settled down on the floor in front.

"It's a Thursday," Martin told her.

Lisa nodded her head with a shrug and thought for a moment. "You know what, that's okay, I think we'll do it anyway, what do you think?"

"I think *you* are going to have a lot of people coming from out of town," Martin reminded her. He was a little disappointed because he knew she was right about having it no matter what day of the week it fell on.

Lisa bit her lip. She didn't know what to say. He was right that she was going to have a lot of people from home coming up here and probably needing to stay which would mean they would have to take two days off of work.

Martin went over to her and put his hands on her shoulders and looked into her eyes. "I know you liked the idea but we can still have a Valentine's wedding can't we?" he asked. "On the Friday or Saturday, it's within two days."

Lisa looked at the calendar. She knew right away that it didn't matter if her wedding anniversary fell right on February fourteenth, it was just the idea. It was easy enough to carry the same theme through to the weekend. She started to nod and then she wondered if her ideas for the day would have been any different anyway.

"So?" Martin asked looking for a verdict.

Lisa nodded slowly. "We could try for the Saturday but there might be a lot of others who were looking to do the same thing," she replied.

Martin nodded again in agreement. "So then we pick Friday."

Lisa decided in the end to call her family and ask them which day would suit them better and the answers were all the same: they'd rather only have to take one day off work.

Martin didn't have very many people to call as most of his friends no longer stayed in contact with him since he'd moved so most of his friends were already in the area and were retired.

They settled for trying to book a few things for the Saturday but would settle for Friday if they couldn't. They also decided that if they had the reception at the house, then they wouldn't have to worry about booking a hall which would probably be really booked up.

They set everything aside for the moment and Martin pulled Lisa close to him and kissed her. They stayed that way for quite some time before Martin pulled away and offered to take her to bed. He made sure the fire was out before he helped her off the floor and they went upstairs.

They made love before Martin pulled her close and watched as she went to sleep.

CHAPTER 18

Martin woke the next morning. He couldn't sleep any longer and he had a bit of a kink in his neck. He rubbed it with the thought he must have slept wrong as he went downstairs. He didn't look at a clock until he got to the kitchen and stifled a yawn. He raised his eyebrows at the fact he'd slept until 9:05 and proceeded to make some coffee. While that was brewing, he pulled the phone book close to him and called his church. The church secretary had just walked in the door and had to put him on hold so she could remove her coat. When she came back on the line, he asked the obvious question.

"The Saturday after Valentine's?" she asked.

"That's right," Martin replied anxiously tapping his fingers on the countertop in front of him.

"Give me just one sec," she replied. "I just have to get that calendar out from under this years," she said in a somewhat surprising tone.

Martin held his tongue but wanted to ask why this seemed to be buried so far away considering the New Year was three months away.

"February," she said into the phone as if trying to remember what order the months of the year went in. "Oh yes, here we are," she finally said.

Martin rolled his eyes. He reminded her who was calling as he knew there was no fee for the church itself for members. "We're looking at the sixteenth," he said.

"The sixteenth, right here, actually there's nothing going on that day," she told him.

"Really?" he asked. "That's great. Can you put me down for a wedding?" he asked.

"Certainly, do you know what time?" she asked.

"Not yet but if you do have someone else asking can you please call me. We should know very soon."

She jotted down his name and number as she asked him for the information and then connected him to the minister.

"Ah yes, just the man I was waiting to hear from," the minister said after Martin had said who was calling.

"Why is that?" Martin asked.

"Well, you had a beautiful young woman with you on Sunday who was wearing a very sparkly ring on a very important finger. When were you planning for?"

Martin was only slightly annoyed that the minister was cocky enough to believe that Martin would, in fact, be getting in touch with him but sloughed it off for the time being and proceeded to tell him the date.

"That's fine with me," the minister replied after he too seemed to have to search all over for his calendar.

"That's great, it won't be long before we work out a time and I'll let you know as soon as I know," he explained.

"No rush, no rush, it's all good," the minister replied. "Of course I'd like to sit down with the two of you at some point but we'll get to that."

Martin said goodbye as quickly as he could and got up to pour himself a cup of coffee before he proceeded to the

Yellow Pages to find out who else he may need to be calling. He came across a section titled *Weddings* and thought he'd start there. When he saw the listings there he groaned. *All that?* He asked himself. He jotted down a few things and then went backwards in search of those particular services, especially of those businesses that paid to have their ad in only one part of the phone book rather than two. He couldn't resist calling his one favourite hall to see if it was at all possible to get it but it was, as he assumed, already booked.

"Guess the reception *is* here," he said out loud.

"Works for me," Lisa said coming into the kitchen.

"You got me back for scaring you the other day," as Martin looked up and smiled. He loved looking at her all the time, even in the morning when her hair was everywhere and she had little lines on her face from where her cheek had pressed against the pillow.

Lisa's smile was warm in return and she went and helped herself to a cup of coffee before she joined him at the breakfast bar. "So what are you doing?" she asked.

He told her the church was available on the Saturday and that it was up to her what time they had the ceremony at.

She thought about for a few moments. "Leave that with me," she replied. "I'm debating."

He also told her that he had called his one favourite hall in town and it was in fact booked that night. "That's as far as I got," he told her.

"Well that's okay, I see you've made a list though," she said trying to read his writing upside down.

"I started, I've written down things that we need like flowers and a photographer."

Lisa nodded. "I don't know a whole lot about these things, just what I've seen when I've been to friends' weddings."

"Same here. Now how about some breakfast?" he asked as he stood and stretched.

"Been up long?" Lisa asked.

"No, not at all actually, that's all I got done," he replied as he thought for a moment then put the cereal on the counter and laughed at the raised eyebrow he got from Lisa. He shrugged. "Not in the mood for much else."

Lisa laughed and waited for a bowl before she filled it with cereal, topped it with milk and proceeded to eat it.

Martin did the same after he sat down and he continued to make his list as Lisa spoke.

They exchanged ideas on what they would do with the house for the reception to be held there. It wasn't going to hold a lot of people and there was no way they could put a tent in the back.

"Maybe we should have gone with your idea of waiting until the summer," Martin said.

"We still can," Lisa replied and sighed. She just didn't know, and in some ways, she didn't care at the same time. She definitely wanted to marry Martin, it just wasn't one of her priorities since she was already living with him.

"I think we should just keep it small, what we can handle," he replied.

After breakfast they moved down the list until they had reached the end and had everyone tentatively booked for February.

Lisa called home to tell her mother that it was the sixteenth. Her mother wasn't impressed that it was going to be in the middle of the winter and started asking about bad weather and all that. Lisa tried to ward off the ongoing bitching but it wasn't helping at all. Then Lisa heard her father's voice and he came on the line. "Lisa, I'm so sorry about your mother," he said.

"Hi dad," Lisa started. "Ask this of mom sometime will you, how come she wanted me to get married and have kids so badly and now that I am she's raining on my parade?" she asked.

Lisa's father was silent for a few minutes before he answered. "I think she thought you'd never move away and now a simple vacation has brought this on."

"I didn't plan it," she said sheepishly.

"I know you didn't, in life we never know where it's going to take us, your mother doesn't understand that."

"I think she better start," Lisa said, "or she might never meet the grandchildren she wants so badly."

"I understand you're frustrated. Can we talk about it when you're here for Thanksgiving?" her father tried desperately to iron things out for the time being.

"Yeah, by then I'll know everything that's going on. I can't wait to see you dad," she told him.

"Same here. You're not *that* far away you know," he replied.

"I know, but tell that to mom."

This time he laughed at what she had to say and they hung up shortly after.

"Sounds like your dad's the peacekeeper," Martin said as she set the phone down.

Lisa nodded. "Yeah, that's about right. Don't know what keeps him there though," she added.

"True love," Martin stated. "Shall we go shower?"

"Yes, we shall and then we should get on the road to go and meet Anna."

Martin nodded. He'd been thinking about that and wondering what would happen if Anna wanted to come to the place she was born. He realized they'd cross that bridge later on.

They went to shower and made love there and towelled each other off, which had almost become their morning routine. They both made the bed and tidied up the bedroom and Martin started a load of laundry.

"Are you ready for this?" Martin asked as they put their jackets on.

Lisa picked up her purse. "As ready as I can be," she replied.

They went out to the van and drove the short drive into town and since Martin knew his way around he found it with little problem.

When they got inside, it was a flurry of activity. They approached the desk and asked an older woman where they could find Anna Shantz. They were quickly given directions to her room but then the woman stopped. "No, wait, Anna, almost 11:00 a.m. would be in the games room just finishing playing her daily round of Euchre. She's the best we have that one," they were told.

Martin and Lisa smiled at each other and thanked her graciously. Regretting not getting directions to the games room, they followed the others heading in the direction the woman had pointed and figured they had to be going the right way. Everyone turned left and so did they, and soon they saw a large green sign with a deck of cards fanned out across the top, two crib boards down each side and what appeared to be some crokinole pieces along the bottom. The two words they were looking for were spelled out in the middle with a piece from just about any game you could imagine including Monopoly money. They smiled at someone's creativeness and followed the crowd inside.

"Must be something new starting at eleven," Martin said.

"Judging by this crowd, I'd have to say you're right," Lisa agreed. "How do you think we'll find her?"

Martin scanned the room. Everyone they had been following had lined up around the outside of the room. In the middle sat an elderly woman, a cane propped up on the table beside her, and three elderly gentlemen who all looked pretty worried. "I think that would be her," he said pointing in the direction of the game going on in the middle of the room.

Lisa looked and a smile spread across her face and she nodded. "I have to agree that's her."

They watched as the game ended and Anna stood, triumphant and announced to the group that she now desperately needed a drink and she could be found in the bar. Everyone laughed and Martin and Lisa looked at each other.

"Must be a standing joke for her," Lisa suggested.

Martin nodded. "With that reaction, I'd think so."

"Are you two going to stay in my way until I die?"

Martin and Lisa hadn't realized they were still standing in front of the door and that Anna had walked the distance to the door.

"Um, no, sorry, we are looking for you though," Lisa told her.

"You're lookin' for me? What for?" Anna asked.

Lisa smiled. "Because we have something to share with you."

Anna eyeballed Lisa up and down and met Lisa's eyes. "What about?" she asked.

"Sophia," Martin said quietly.

Anna became very quiet and stepped between them. "Follow me," she told them.

They followed her out of the games room and down the same corridor they'd just followed the crowd through. They thought she was taking them to her room but then she turned down another hall away from the rooms and they walked into a quiet room, walls lined with books and huge, overstuffed armchairs everywhere. The room was empty and Anna pointed at two of the chairs indicating they take a seat. They did as they were expected and waited patiently for Anna to sit down across from them.

"So what do you know about Sophia?" she asked.

Martin began by telling the story of how he'd come to acquire the house overlooking the lake. It had already been turned into a B&B.

Lisa filled her in on her vacation plans and how she ended up at the B&B.

They went on, taking turns, describing the voice they'd heard, the appearance of the light and eventually Martin's dream as well as the way to the attic where they'd come across Sophie's things, all packed into a single trunk.

Anna had tears in her eyes as they went on to describe how they'd come to find the small carriage and when they handed it to her, the floodgates opened and the tears flowed freely. All she kept saying was *Oh my God* and Lisa moved to the chair beside and took her hand.

"I went and saw Sheryl, I didn't know who she was, I was looking at making some career changes and happened to connect the name. She told me the story and I asked if I could come see you," Lisa told her.

Anna only nodded. "I'd like to see the place," she said and looked up. "If that's okay."

Martin couldn't resist the old woman's request. "What do we do to bust you out of here?" he asked.

Anna smiled through her tears. "It's a retirement residence, I just leave."

They laughed which helped to break the tension a little and Anna left them in the library to go to her room to get her purse and jacket.

"Wow, what do you think about that?" Martin asked looking intently at Lisa to make sure she was okay.

"I think it was definitely overwhelming," Lisa replied. "What do you think she'll do when she sees the rest of her mother's things?"

"I think she'll do about the same as she did with that carriage. I feel so sorry for her. I can't imagine living almost 80 years of my life believing someone to be my mother to find out that she was never my mother. And what was her father thinking hiding that from her for all that time?" Martin was angry now. He was trying so hard to control it but it had just hit home all the repercussions this had on what had once been a small child.

"We'll never truly know what he was thinking." Lisa was a little scared, she'd never seen this side of Martin before. She realized she wasn't afraid *of* him, and was, in a way, grateful that she finally saw another side of him.

Anna returned, a winter coat on, holding a pair of gloves and a purse hanging from the arm that held her cane.

Lisa smiled. She was sure Anna didn't get out much and that she must think it was extremely cold outside because of the time of year. They led her out to the van and Lisa helped her into the front seat while she took the back.

It was on the trip back to the house that Anna finally asked about the two of them and they started to tell their short story. Anna was in tears again by the time she reached the house and after they'd helped her out of the car and each held a hand that she took hold of them and looked at them both.

"Don't ever let anything that happened in this house come between the two of you," she said sternly. "You are two wonderful people and I can tell you're made for each other."

Lisa and Martin looked at each other and nodded in response to what she said before they led her inside.

Anna's tears continued once inside. They slid silently, in a steady flow, down each cheek the whole time they helped her out of her coat.

"I can feel her," Anna said as she looked around.

Lisa understood what was going on. Sophia was making herself known to Anna because her baby was home at last.

Martin shook his head and went to make them some lunch. He was a little overwhelmed. He wanted to understand how all this stuff worked but he wished he knew now so he could possibly get a little insight into what was happening in his home right now.

Lisa took Anna by the hand and gave her a tour of the house. She explained that the layout of the upstairs wasn't an exact replica of what it was 87 years before but that it was close. She only showed her the door behind which the stairs to the attic stood and then took her back downstairs to the dining room. "This is what we found when we got up there."

Anna sat in one of the chairs and handled each item as if it were going to fall to pieces in her hands. The birth certificate, the marriage license, the obituary, the newspaper articles that Lisa had printed from the library and the items she'd taken from the internet. It was when Lisa handed over the nightgown that Anna truly fell apart.

Lisa went to her and put her arms around her. She didn't know what to say so she just remained a presence. She couldn't begin to imagine how overwhelming this had to be.

Anna finally spoke. "I can't believe all this stuff has been here for all this time," she said. "You know, when my father first called me to see him, I didn't want to go. We'd had a falling out a number of years before, that doesn't really matter, and I had told him I never wanted to see him again. When they told me he was dying and that he only had a few days to live, I had to go. I felt I had received a little push from whom I can only assume was Sophia now and I went. I sat beside him and in a stony silence, listened to everything he had to say. I became less responsive as he went on. I couldn't believe my ears. I couldn't believe I had lived in the same house with the same man who was telling me all this, that this man had been allowed to father a child. I said an icy goodbye and I walked out of the room. I heard he died within the hour but I didn't care anymore. I didn't go to the funeral, I couldn't. Not after that."

Martin interrupted only to bring in the soup he'd made for lunch along with some fresh bread and tea.

Anna was grateful to be served in such a manner and complimented the chef before she continued after Lisa had asked about Meredith.

"Meredith was never cruel to me. She was a little distant as I grew up but I thought that was maybe just me and the idea of having a teenager in the house," she chuckled then had some of her lunch. "She loved me so much and I took it for granted but I loved her too. I never understood where I got my looks from but I never asked either. She died several years before my father, she had cancer, and I had stopped speaking to my father before then so I paid my respects at the funeral home but never went to her funeral either."

Martin and Lisa watched her in silence as she ate her food. Neither knew what to say.

Anna kept looking at the other end of the table where the rest of her mother's things sat laid out like they were fragile. She was dying to get a look at them and she wanted them so badly. "Were there any pictures?" she asked.

Lisa nodded. "There are a number of little things in that shoebox," she said pointing to the only one she'd left on the table. "There were some photos of a baby, I'm assuming that's you."

They talked quietly through lunch and Anna asked them when their big day was and they explained their plans.

"It sounds wonderful," she told them.

Lisa looked at Martin imploringly, hoping beyond hope he'd understand what she was trying to say.

He nodded at her and gave her a wink. "Would you like to come?" he asked.

Anna put both hands to her face. "I'd love to," she said.

Martin cleared away the dishes while Anna moved back to the other end of the dining room and allowed Lisa to continue showing what had come out of the trunk. They assumed the one gown to have been Sophia's wedding gown and they speculated who would have packed her things into the trunk.

"It may have been her parents," Lisa said. Especially if your father was running off with someone else."

"It may have been Isaac feeling sorry for himself and needing to appear like he gave a damn," Anna said.

Lisa nodded. "I don't know what other family there was, the obituary mentioned a sister but it sounds like she had moved away with her husband."

Anna closed her eyes and just took in her surroundings. The essence her mother had left behind and her presence in the room. "She never left here waiting all these years for me to come back to her," she said. "She desperately wanted me to know the truth. My father never even told me this house existed. I've passed it over the years but I never thought anything of it and certainly didn't have a reason to stay here."

Lisa laughed softly. "I guess that's why everyone was saying this place was haunted."

Anna kept her eyes closed as if finally reconnecting with her mother. She started talking, as if having a conversation and Lisa quietly went to the kitchen.

"What's going on? Who's she talking to?" Martin asked.

"She's talking to her mother," Lisa replied.

Martin looked at her skeptically. "I really wish I understood all this stuff," he said.

"I will try my best to explain it all to you when Anna has gone home, okay?" she asked.

They listened to some of what Anna was saying, wondering what was being said on the other side but pretty certain they could probably figure it out if they tried hard enough. Anna was crying again and it was all they could do to just stay where they were and listen and watch.

"What do you think will happen now?" Martin asked.

"I think Anna will probably come here again and then I think she'll write one more novel before she dies," Lisa answered.

"That's quite a prediction," Martin told her and squeezed her tight. He leaned down and kissed her. "Any regrets?" he asked.

Lisa shook her head. "None. How can I regret bringing an 87-year-old woman to a mother she never knew she had? I think that's my good deed for life."

"I think you have a lot of good deeds to go," Martin said giving her a squeeze. "And you can't leave me yet."

Lisa smiled. She had no intentions of leaving him.

It was a long time after lunch that Anna finally called out to Lisa to come back into the room. Martin was making some more tea and gave her a nod to go in to Anna.

"That was quite the conversation you had," Lisa said sitting down.

Anna nodded quietly. "We had a few things to square away," she said.

It was obvious she had been crying. Her face was blotchy and wet, her nose was red and she squeezed a tissue tightly in her hand.

"I bet you did," Lisa replied reaching for the old woman's aging hand. Lined with years of use.

"She's proud of me," Anna said. "I've never had anyone tell me that."

"Somebody has to be proud of you," Lisa said.

"You're right, my husband was proud of me," Anna replied. "And my kids and grandkids are but it's nothing like a mother's."

Lisa nodded. She wished her mother was proud of her getting on with her life.

As if she knew, Anna asked about Lisa's family and the conversation started to turn in the direction of what had brought Lisa here and what Lisa would be doing before and after the wedding.

Anna told Lisa she was proud of her, even if nobody else was.

Lisa had tears in her eyes this time and she thanked Anna quietly just as Martin brought a tray of tea in.

Anna was again delighted by his mannerisms and winked at Lisa as if to say she had made a good choice.

While they had tea, Anna finally opened up about her books and writing career. She told Lisa she was going to give her a complete set of her books with the hopes it would give her some incentive to write and Lisa replied that they would also satisfy her need for reading material.

They took Anna home just before supper after Lisa had showed her all the remaining items that were there. Anna took the shoebox filled with papers with her as she wanted to go through them one by one. She said she'd like to take the rest of the items but didn't have room at the home for them all but she did take the nightgown with her as well. She seemed drawn to the small carriage and held it all the way back to the home. They took her inside and led her back inside. This time she invited them to her room where they waited while she took her coat off and tucked her purse away in the drawer of her nightstand. She cleared away a spot on a dresser and set the shoebox there along with the nightgown. Again she didn't let go of the carriage.

She turned to them, again tears coming to her eyes. "I can't thank you enough," she said.

"We did what we had to do," Lisa said.

"You didn't ever have to tell me," she said. "You are wonderful people." She reached for them and gave them both a hug and held them there for quite some time. "I will see you again?"

"Of course you will, you want to come back out to the house right?" Martin confirmed.

"Oh yes, and I hope you'll go back up to the attic and see if there's anything else up there," she said.

Lisa nodded, "I will do my best," she promised.

"Plus you're coming to the wedding right?" Martin asked.

"I wouldn't miss it for the world," Anna replied with a smile. "Now I better get to dinner. Walk me to the dining room?" she asked.

They nodded at her and each took an arm and let her lead the way.

"Smells great," Martin commented as they neared her destination.

"Ah, forget that, they never use enough salt," Anna replied now sounding more like an 87-year-old.

They both laughed. "Salt isn't that good for you," Martin told her.

"I've lived this long, why can't I eat what I want?" she asked.

"They want you to live a little longer," Lisa replied.

They all laughed again and she gave them each a kiss on the cheek and one last thank-you before she disappeared to her table.

As they left, they could almost hear Anna telling anyone who would listen what had happened to her that afternoon and who the strangers were who had just shown up and taken her from the home.

Martin and Lisa smiled as they walked out the door and instead of driving home, Martin drove around the corner to their favourite restaurant but when they realized they weren't dressed appropriately, they went next door instead.

They discussed the events of the afternoon and Lisa tried to explain what she knew about the *other world* and how things worked.

Martin didn't totally get it but he understood a bit more of what had probably happened in his home that afternoon.

When they got home, hours later, it was quiet and dark as they'd forgotten to turn on some lights. But when Lisa went into the den to turn on a lamp, she noticed the corner of the room was glowing and she called to Martin.

He came in and almost crashed into her. "That's Sophia," he said.

The light flickered once and Lisa said hello. The light only flickered again. They both stood, uncertain of what else they could do and then the light flickered twice.

"I think she's saying thank you," Lisa said.

When the light flickered once more, Lisa was sure that's what she was trying to say.

"We're going to bring her back here again," Lisa told Sophia.

The light flickered once more at her.

"Soon," Martin said. "Is there something more we need to get for her?"

Lisa looked up at him. *Good question,* she thought.

The light flickered repeatedly as if excited and Lisa knew she had to keep her promise about getting back up the attic.

Another slip of paper shot across the room at them and then a voice finally. "Thank you." The light dimmed and Lisa reached out to turn on the lamp she'd intended to turn on when she'd first entered the room.

Lisa turned the paper over and again there was a drawing of the attic, this time with an *X* in a different spot. "There's more up there," she said.

"Can we watch a really funny movie and just forget about this for now?" Martin asked.

Lisa smiled. "Yeah, let's do that."

Martin went to the kitchen to make popcorn while Lisa picked a DVD from his collection and slid it into the DVD player.

They sat and watched the movie, spilling popcorn and laughing. When it was over, Martin picked Lisa up and carried her upstairs where he made love to her repeatedly until she cried out telling him to stop. Then it was his turn and all he wanted to do was hold her, love her and be with her for all of eternity yet he knew with their age difference that wouldn't be possible so he vowed he would make it all as great as he could.

CHAPTER 19

The months flew by and it was the week of the wedding. Martin and Lisa were visiting Anna on a regular basis and bringing her to stay at the house every now and again.

They had made it to Waterloo for a tense Thanksgiving celebration with her family. Her mother didn't totally approve of her daughter's choice and was told to shut up by Lisa's brother. They had also celebrated her birthday while she was there as her birthday was two days after the holiday.

Lisa had to go back to work the day after so they couldn't stay all day on the holiday but did get to the parade.

Martin met Lisa at work on Wednesday and took her out for dinner at their favourite restaurant and while they were on the dance floor Lisa pulled Martin close to her, took his hand in hers and set it on her stomach and whispered in his ear. "I'm pregnant."

Martin was ecstatic and asked her over and over if she was feeling alright. He took her home and sat her down and asked her to tell him again.

"I'll need to go to the doctor to find out my due date but it should be sometime next June," she told him.

"You need a doctor here," he said. "I'll call mine tomorrow morning."

Lisa giggled. She couldn't believe how excited he was. She knew he wouldn't be upset but she didn't think he would be this excited.

She'd settled in at work and Pete was only a little upset she was pregnant. She was only part time so it wasn't like he couldn't cover the position while she was off. They had also told Anna who was elated by the news as well and wanted to know every detail every time Lisa had been to the doctor.

Christmas was tense as well with her mother she was glad she wasn't showing yet as she still couldn't bring herself to tell her family to save herself from the wrath of her mother.

Martin took her to Bayfield again for New Year's where they again stayed at the B&B there much to Maria's delight and when she found out Lisa was pregnant she wouldn't let her do a single thing.

Now, with only a few days to go, Lisa was getting frazzled and Martin was trying to calm her down. She was getting bigger and the fact that she couldn't do everything she wanted to do was getting her down.

"Stop worrying," Martin had tried to reassure her.

"I'm going to be so fat," she said.

"You're going to look fabulous, in fact you do look fabulous," he tried telling her.

Lisa wouldn't listen to him. When she went to try on her gown though, she found they'd done a wonderful job of altering it to suit her slightly larger tummy and they complimented her on how great she looked.

"You would never know you're five months along," the woman told her.

Lisa calmed down a little after that but not for long. Her mother was arriving and she was determined that everything would be perfect.

They had cleaned all the rooms up for her family to stay in and Martin had booked a room with Maria again for their wedding night.

Martin pulled Lisa into the dining room, sat her down and made her eat the wonderful roast he'd cooked. She finally relaxed and after they'd finished eating he led her to the den where he stretched her out on the couch and rubbed her feet. That led to his hands wandering up her legs and before too long he was pulling her onto the floor where he made love to her.

Lisa cried out, releasing all the tension she'd been saving up in her body and fell asleep in Martin's arms.

It was a couple hours later when he woke her and carried her up to bed where it was her turn to reach out to him and they made love again, once more caressing each other and bringing each other pleasure beyond the norm.

Almost everything was in order for the wedding and then the phone rang. It was the retirement home and as soon as Lisa saw the number on the caller ID she handed it to Martin. "I can't answer that," she said, obviously fearful.

Martin took the phone uncertain that he wanted to answer it either. "Hello?" he asked almost in a whisper.

"Uh-huh," he said as Lisa looked at him with a horrified look on her face. She unconsciously crossed her fingers and squeezed her eyes shut saying a prayer.

"Okay, thank you," Martin said followed by a goodbye. He set the phone down and turned to look at Lisa. "Anna was taken to the hospital," he told her.

"Is she alright?" Lisa asked. Anna's health had deteriorated since they'd met her. Lisa assumed it was because her life's journey was almost complete. All the time she'd spent at the house with them getting to know her mother as best she could had drained her of her energies. She had managed to write that one last book too which was going to be published in the spring.

"Apparently she started having trouble breathing. They took her in by ambulance, they think she may be having a heart attack."

Lisa sucked in a breath. "I hope not," she said. "I really wanted her to be here."

"So did I sweetie, so did I." Martin put his arms around her and held her tight. "Should we get down there, see what's going on?"

Lisa nodded into his chest, tears welling up in her eyes like a dam getting ready to burst.

"Then let's go."

They slid into boots and coats as the cold weather and snow was certainly upon them and they locked up the house and left. The roads were dry so it was an easy drive into town and Martin made a mental list on the way of a few other things that needed to be done while they were in town including stocking up on several days worth of groceries in order to feed all who were coming.

It didn't take long before they arrived and Martin parked the car and they went inside. They approached the emergency desk and asked for Anna Shantz.

"She's in the x-ray department right now," they were told by the nurse. "Are you family?"

Lisa looked at her. "Almost, she's kind of adopted us over the last few months."

Martin nodded beside her.

"Then just have a seat, you can see her as soon as she comes back. She's stable."

Lisa was relieved to learn that much and she didn't want to push for more information.

They turned towards the waiting area and saw Sheryl sitting by herself. They went over to her and asked her how her grandmother was.

Sheryl shrugged her shoulders. "They needed to do tests first so they haven't told me anything."

Lisa looked at Martin. Sheryl hadn't warmed up to Lisa, in fact she'd only become icier when she found out Lisa and Martin had befriended the old woman and taken her to the house.

"Where's your mom?" Lisa asked trying to make small talk.

"She and my dad went on a cruise, I've tried to call, with no luck, but if I don't have anything to tell them then there's not much point right now," she said.

Martin pointed at a chair and told Lisa she should sit down.

Lisa nodded and sat down, putting her purse on her lap.

"Oh yeah, I heard that your pregnant, congratulations," Sheryl said even more sarcastically than she'd said anything else.

"Uh, thanks," Lisa said.

Just then a stretcher rolled by and they glimpsed Anna's white hair poking out and Lisa jumped back out of her chair and went over. "Anna," she called.

"Is that Lisa?" Anna asked from behind an oxygen mask.

"Yes, I'm right here," Lisa said.

Sheryl scowled in the background. "I'm here too grandma," she said from behind Martin.

"We need to get her back into a room," the staff that was with her said.

"The nurse said we could see her when she came back," Lisa said.

"By all means, we have to wait for the results which won't take too long but we'll be in to talk to everyone as soon as we know."

They followed the stretcher through the emergency doors and into a long room, partitioned only by curtains. The nurse pulled the curtain around the bed to allow them some privacy for their visit.

"So what happened?" Lisa asked approaching Anna and taking her hand.

Sheryl stood back scowling some more until Anna called her to the other side.

"I just had trouble breathing," she told them. "I couldn't catch my breath."

"They told us when they called they thought you were having a heart attack," Lisa informed her.

"That's what they've been testing me for I think," she replied.

It seemed like forever before someone finally came in and when he did, he made a point of introducing himself as Anna's doctor.

"So what's the verdict?" Martin asked as it seemed he was the only one in the room not holding his breath.

"We did a chest CT which shows some leakage of one of the valves which is causing the breathing problem," he started. "Because of the fluid leakage, it backs up into the lungs."

"Is there anything you can do?" Lisa asked.

"We can repair it," he said.

Lisa let go of the breath she didn't even realize she'd been holding.

"We'll get her lined up for surgery on Monday morning," he told her. "The sooner the better."

"Can she go home until then?" Lisa asked.

The doctor looked at her.

"She has an invitation to our wedding on Saturday afternoon," she told him.

Sheryl had shrunk back and was still holding her grandmother's hand but glared at her grandmother when she heard what Lisa said.

Anna patted Sheryl's hand and looked at the doctor waiting for his answer.

"She can go back to the retirement home, tomorrow and she has to rest until the wedding on Saturday afternoon," he said sternly.

Anna lifted her hand and saluted. "Anything you say young man," she told him, sounding more like her old self.

Everyone laughed, including Sheryl for once. "I better get back to the store though," she said and kissed her grandmother on the cheek.

Lisa turned to look at Anna and smiled. Then she put a hand to her stomach. "I have to sit down."

"Are you okay?" Martin asked.

"I think so," she said slowly.

Anna was looking on with concern. Her breathing becoming rapid. "Get a doctor Martin," she told him.

"For you?" he asked.

"No, for her," Anna said pointing at her. "Something's wrong."

Martin had sheer terror written across his face as he bolted from the room to find someone. They heard him calling down the hall for help.

Everyone seemed to come running at once and started to surround the bed.

"Not me, her," Anna said sternly. "She's five months pregnant and she may be having contractions."

They swooped her away in a wheelchair so fast Martin wasn't sure what to do. He looked to Anna.

"Go with her, I'm staying overnight anyway. Just keep me posted," she called after him as he shot out from behind the curtain again.

He followed the staff to the elevator and jumped on with them. He had no idea where he was going so he stayed close behind. The elevator stopped and they all got off and turned left down the corridor marked *Obstetrics*.

Nurses came running from everywhere and were told what was going on.

They took it from there and the staff from downstairs walked back to the elevator wishing Martin good luck as they passed him.

He ran into the room where they had taken her and were helping her into a gown. She looked at him with fear in her eyes and he wanted so desperately to go to her.

The staff left them alone for a moment after they'd put her in bed and attached a monitor to her from which they could hear the baby's heart beat but there was something else there as well.

A doctor came in. "Hi Lisa, what's going on?" she asked as she rounded the bed and looked at all the markings on the tape and watched as Lisa again held a hand to her stomach.

"I don't know," Lisa replied.

"I need to examine you, is it okay for him to be in the room?" the doctor asked in reference to Martin.

"Yes, it's fine," Lisa told her. "He's the father."

The doctor pulled the sheet back, helped Lisa to position her legs and proceeded to check her. "Okay, everything is fine there," she said.

Lisa sighed with relief.

"Well it's not that easy," the doctor continued as she put the sheet back over her legs.

Martin went and sat on the edge of the bed and took Lisa's hand in his own.

"You're having contractions, and strong enough ones to start labour. You're fine right now but we do need to start an IV and get some medication into you that will stop them completely."

Lisa and Martin nodded together.

"Do what you have to," Martin told her as Lisa nodded beside him.

The doctor left and a few moments later a nurse came in with the IV supplies and proceeded to insert the IV and started the drip explaining everything as she went along.

Lisa and Martin chatted quietly while the IV dripped, every heartbeat of their baby a precious gift to them.

The doctor returned after a half hour and checked the tape again. "Anymore contractions?" she asked Lisa.

Lisa shook her head. "Can I go home?" she asked.

"You can soon. The drip is done and it seems to have worked but we like to keep our patients in overnight just to monitor and make sure it actually works. Then you're on bedrest."

They both looked at her.

"We're getting married on Saturday," Martin said.

The doctor raised an eyebrow. "Okay, then we keep her overnight and give her another dose of this before she goes home tomorrow. But Sunday she's back in bed."

They nodded in agreement, resigned to the fact they had no choice.

She spoke with them for a little longer, thrilled they were getting married and assuming that it was the added stress from the wedding plans that had caused the premature labour.

When Martin explained what had happened to Anna, the doctor agreed completely that that incident was the one that had pushed Lisa over.

She left then to leave the instructions with the nursing staff and wished them well.

"I better go downstairs and put Anna's mind at rest," Martin said. "If that's okay with you."

Lisa nodded. "If you don't, it may worsen her condition," she replied.

Martin kissed her, then held her, then kissed her again. "I love you so much. Please take care of our baby."

"I love you too. And I'm so scared."

"Just relax or you'll make it worse, please," Martin pleaded.

Lisa nodded. "I'll try but I'd be happier at home."

"I know, but we need to do what they say," he told her.

Lisa sucked in a breath, resigned to the fact that everything was going to go wrong before the wedding.

Martin left the room and went in search of Anna. He went back to where they'd left her only to be told by the staff there that she'd been transferred to a room. They gave him the floor and room number and he left to find her.

"Martin," she said as he walked in the door. "How's Lisa? What happened? What's wrong?" she asked.

"Okay, slow down, Lisa's fine. She started having contractions so they've given her some medication to stop them and so far it's worked but she has to stay overnight now and give her more in the morning before she goes home."

Anna sighed. "She's not out of the woods is she?" she asked.

Martin shook her head. "No, she's not. She has to stay in bed until the wedding on Saturday and then right back into bed on Sunday."

"This is all my fault I'm afraid," Anna said. She grabbed Martin's hand. "I'm so sorry, please tell Lisa I'm so sorry."

"It's not all your fault," Martin reassured her. "It was the planning of the wedding that's had her really stressed out."

Anna nodded. She had forgotten about that part for a short time.

"I need to get back to her though," Martin said.

"I know you do dear," Anna said. "Off you go."

Martin kissed her cheek and gave her hand a squeeze. "You get some rest so you can come to the wedding on Saturday."

Anna gave him a salute this time and shooed him out of the room.

Martin went back to Lisa's room where he found her resting with her head back and her eyes closed, tears silently rolling down her cheeks. He walked over to the bed and slid his hand in hers. "Don't cry," he said.

She opened her eyes and looked up at him. "I am so scared."

He sat on the side of the bed and took her into his arms. He held her and rocked her until she had stopped crying. "Listen to me," he said in her ear. "You are fine and the baby is fine. Listen to the heart beating over there." He stopped so she could listen. "You need to relax or there *won't* be a baby."

Lisa pulled away and looked up at him.

"I'm going to try."

"Then settle back and I'll talk to you until you fall asleep," he told her.

She did her best to get settled and then he started talking quietly to her. Telling her to take deep breaths and let her eyes clothes and fall asleep. He told her he would take care of the rest of the wedding arrangements and she was to sit back and relax.

Finally she was asleep and he left the room to go to the cafeteria. He sat down with a cup of coffee and took deep breaths himself, trying to relax so he could be there for the woman and baby he loved.

He said a silent prayer for Lisa, the baby and Anna. He knew how important it was to Lisa for Anna to be at the wedding and he also knew she wanted Anna to at least be able to see the baby after it was born. They were desperately racing against time though as Anna was soon to turn 88.

A nurse he vaguely recognized was crossing the cafeteria, scanning the tables and then she came straight at him. "Martin?" she asked.

"Yes?" he said.

"Good, I was hoping I'd recognize you," she said. "Your wife is looking for you."

"Oh, okay, thank you," he said and rose out of his chair. He picked up his cup and followed her back upstairs.

"What's up?" he asked when he walked into the room.

Lisa was tearing up again and motioned for him to come sit with her.

He sat on the bed and took her hand in his. "What is it?" he asked.

She took his hand and pressed it against her stomach and smiled as she watched him smile once he felt the baby kick.

His eyes opened wide and he looked at her questioningly. Then he smiled when she nodded.

"I'm going to go home soon, it's been a long day and you need to get some rest too so you can come home tomorrow," Martin said.

"I wish you didn't have to go," she said.

"I know, it will be the first night we've spent apart." He kissed her long and hard. "I'm going to miss you terribly," he whispered.

"Me too and I'm probably not going to sleep very well here either."

"Do your best. You can come home and rest in bed all day tomorrow," he promised. "I'll keep you company."

Lisa nodded. "Okay."

Martin kissed her goodbye and left the room. He got on the elevator but didn't leave right away. Instead he had one more stop to make.

"Hey, I thought you'd gone home," Anna said.

"I was on my way out and thought I'd check on you one last time. Lisa's staying and getting ready to go to sleep," he said. "She's had a tough day too."

"I'm afraid that's my fault," Anna said.

"Don't blame yourself," Martin told her. "We were probably lucky it happened here and not at home."

Anna met his eyes. "I can't help but think that this is still my fault though," she said again.

Martin leaned down and gave her a peck on the cheek. "Please don't think that," he said. "She'll be okay. You just keep yourself healthy because it's extremely important to Lisa that you be there on Saturday."

"I have every intention of being there Saturday."

They hugged and Martin left feeling like his heart was in his shoes. The woman he loved had to stay here, he would spend the first night away from her since she'd arrived and he felt part of it was his fault because he had suggested the wedding be around Valentine's Day. Had they kept her suggestion, she would have had the baby before the wedding. He had to make Saturday as easy as possible for her and he knew he would have to check her lists and be sure to run as many of the errands as he could.

He got in the car, his heart heavy, and drove home. It felt so lonely when he walked in the front door and a tear came to his eye. The realization he could have lost his baby hit home and he turned out the lights and went upstairs. He lay on the bed and cried for a while. The thoughts of what all could have happened running through his mind. Thoughts of not only losing the baby but also losing Lisa, the love of his life he'd waited far too long for. He couldn't bear the thought and the tears fell freely. It was quite some time before he got up, brushed his teeth and crawled between the sheets. It didn't take him long to fall asleep as he was exhausted but his dreams were constant with all the terrible endings he had been thinking of.

It was six when he woke and decided to get up. He wasn't going to sleep anymore so he showered and dressed and went downstairs for some breakfast. He wasn't very hungry so he decided to have some coffee and a couple slices of toast. He knew it was too early to go to the hospital so he checked Lisa's lists for what needed to be done over the next couple of days. Not much needed to be done until at least Thursday, but he thought maybe one or two things could be done before that time. He used different highlighters to mark off the ones he thought he could get done, one being picking up the majority of the flowers as she'd ordered silk for all of the bouquets, she'd only ordered real flowers for the bouquets going to the church.

He needed to see her so he got in the van and drove back to the hospital. He decided to check in on Anna first and she was getting ready to return to the home. He told her he'd give her love to Lisa and they would keep her posted as to how things were going as long as she did the same.

He went upstairs where the small bag holding the medication was dripping slowly into Lisa's arms and her eyes were closed. He heard the now familiar steady beat of the baby's heart and he felt his stomach lurch. There was no way he could lose that baby now, that sound filled him with an intense amount of love he didn't even know he could muster.

"Hey," Lisa said quietly.

"Hey!" he said as he approached the bed and sat down pulling her into his arms and kissing her. "I missed you."

"I missed you too. I want to go home," she said.

"I'm here to see that happens," Martin told her. "I see they're running the drip, can you go home soon?" he asked.

She shrugged her shoulders. "That's what they said yesterday," she told him.

"I know. I'll find out soon. How are you feeling? Any reoccurrences overnight?"

She shook her head. "None, I didn't sleep all that great because I was still scared."

"I doubt there's much to worry about after they've given you this. I'll go find out who's in charge and see if you can get out of here. Anna's already on her way."

Lisa's eyes widened and Martin filled her in before he left the room.

He went to the closest nurse he could find and checked on Lisa's status.

"As soon as her IV is dry, we'll remove it and she can get dressed and go home."

"That's great, I'll tell her. Thanks," he called back as he almost ran down the hall.

It wasn't quite that simple though. The IV finished running and the nurse did come in to remove it but she also did another exam before she gave Lisa some explicit instructions. Finally they were ready to go and Lisa held Martin's hand as they left the room. It wasn't until they reached the elevator that Martin started to grumble.

"We can't have sex until after the baby's born?"

Lisa nodded. "Doctor's orders." She shrugged. She too was extremely disappointed but she was a little more concerned about the baby.

"Whoa," he said.

"We've made love just about every day since we met," she said. "That *is* going to be tough. But I am worried about the baby."

Martin pulled her close. "We'll do whatever we need to do to make sure that baby arrives safely."

Lisa sighed and felt her shoulders drop, unaware she'd been that tense before.

They got on the elevator and made one stop only to find out Anna had already been discharged back to the home and her daughter had picked her up not that long ago.

"Let's get you home to bed," Martin said. "Oh, but we have one stop to make first."

He helped her into the van and he drove towards town rather than away and pulled up outside the flower shop. "I'm picking up the flowers," he told her. "Just the silk ones," he reassured her quickly as she opened her mouth to ask.

Lisa closed her mouth again and stared at him for a moment before he jumped out of the car. *When did I lose control of this?* She wondered. Then she felt the baby kick. *When something went wrong with the pregnancy,* she answered her own question. She set her head back on the headrest and closed her eyes. It had been a long two days in the end and she had a few more difficult ones to go. She was grateful that her family was only coming up on Saturday morning and they weren't coming Friday night to wreak havoc on the remaining planning. They were going to come on Friday if the forecast for Saturday was bad but she'd checked and it was supposed to be clear all weekend and she made a point of saying a little prayer of thank you.

Martin came back out of the store, with the clerk in tow, carrying two boxes each. They slid them all very carefully onto the back seats and Martin stood talking for a few minutes.

Lisa saw him shaking his head and wondered what they were talking about. Finally Martin got in the car. "What was all that about?" she asked.

"She's going to deliver the other bouquets to the church," he said as he started the van again. "You okay?"

"I'm fine," Lisa reassured him. "That was going to cost extra," she added.

"Not anymore. Told her about you and what happened and she's going to deliver them, no charge."

Lisa looked at him and smiled. She couldn't believe him sometimes. He must have been quite the businessman in his time.

"What?" he asked.

She shook her head. "Nothing, you just never cease to amaze me."

He drove her home and got her upstairs and into bed before he unloaded the flowers and placed them on the dining room table. They had finally cleared away all of Sophia's things and he was grateful he had hired a housecleaner to come in and give the place a good once over before the reception messed it all up again on Saturday night. He looked around the room and closed his eyes to imagine how it was going to look. He and Lisa had decided to set up the dining room as a buffet style dinner with as many tables as they could fit spilling into the attached living room. They would then have to clear away some of the tables for a dance floor but it was all going to work out anyway.

He could imagine himself holding Lisa in his arms as he led her around their makeshift dance floor for the first time as husband and wife in front of all their friends. He couldn't wait. It was merely a formality for him and he knew that sounded so catty but it was. She was his already, and he hers for that matter. He loved her and he couldn't love her any more after the wedding than he did at that moment. A woman who had merely been passing through, all that had happened, it truly amazed him. He went and sat down in one of the cozy chairs by the fireplace and felt tears come to his eyes. The nurse had said Lisa would be on bed rest until she saw her doctor. That was the week after the wedding. She had taken the time off from work anyway but they were hoping to get down to Bayfield again and stay with Maria for a night or two. He hoped she'd be able to manage that trip on Saturday night.

Martin finally stood and went to the kitchen where he made tea, pulled out some cookies and carried it all upstairs. He found Lisa in bed, reading a bridal magazine and he smiled. "Little late for that don't you think?" he asked.

"It was all I could reach," she replied. She'd shut it quickly as she had turned to the page where the gown she'd chosen had been featured.

"You should have called me," he told her. He handed her a steaming cup. "Careful."

"I know," she replied sharply. "I'm sorry, I..."

Martin knew what was coming. "It's okay, I understand." He hadn't picked up his own cup yet so he left it and went to her. He took her cup and set it aside so he could pull her into his arms. He rocked her, all the while just whispering into her ear. Finally she calmed down and he pulled away slightly. "It's all going to be fine," he tried again to reassure her.

Lisa nodded. Somewhere deep down she knew it would all be okay, but she'd had such a huge scare. She certainly had never experienced contractions before and when she realized what was going on, she was even more concerned.

They stayed in the bedroom for the rest of the day and watched DVD's on the TV in the room. Martin only left long enough to make supper and bring them snacks. He also brought in the crib board and they played, and watched movies until Lisa finally said she'd had enough and he finally slid into bed beside her and pulled her into his arms wanting desperately to make love to her but also wanting to keep her safe for the rest of his life.

CHAPTER 20

The next morning Martin woke first and went downstairs to make breakfast and with that a pot of tea. He returned to the bedroom just as Lisa was getting back from the bathroom and he set the tray down in time to help her back into bed.

They talked about the rehearsal later on in the day and Lisa's best friend was to arrive later on in the afternoon. *She* had been thrilled that Lisa was getting married and was more than willing to come up and stand up for Lisa.

After breakfast, Martin again cleared everything away and then sat on the bed beside her. He hesitated for only a moment before he kissed her, his lips brushing hers. She felt so wonderful and he deepened the kiss, wanting to hold her, be near her. He wanted to make love to her, but knew he couldn't.

Lisa didn't fight the kiss, or his hands slowly wandering. It felt wonderful to have his hand cupping her breast and she slid it beneath her nighty to allow his skin to touch hers. His lips pressed against hers and she too wanted him to make love to her. Tears came to her eyes as she realized that she couldn't make love until after the baby was born and all she wanted to do was take Martin into her arms and feel him in the way that only two intimate people could feel one another.

"What's wrong?" Martin asked pulling away.

"I want to make love."

Martin nodded. "I want to make love to you more than anything right now," he told her as he took her hand in his and placed over the bulge in his lap.

Instead of making love, they undressed and held onto each other, touching, feeling skin against skin.

"I'd like to take a shower with you," Lisa whispered as she nibbled at his earlobe.

Martin nodded in agreement and pulled her closer to him and his lips pressed harder against hers.

Finally, unable to take anymore, he pulled away and rolled off the other side of the bed and went into the bathroom. He adjusted the water to the right temperature and returned to the bedroom to get Lisa.

Lisa had a smile on her face.

"What?" he asked.

"Nothing, I just want to be really close to you," she told him.

He frowned. What they both wanted to do the most they couldn't and they were doing their best to make the best out of it.

"I'm definitely asking the doctor if they were right or not," Lisa said as Martin helped her ease off the bed and led her into the bathroom where he again helped her into the shower. He joined her a few moments later and pulled her into his arms, holding onto her, kissing her neck, his hands sliding easily over her wet skin.

When they finally agreed they'd had enough of that, they dried each other off and Lisa put on a clean nightgown and, with Martin's help, climbed back into bed.

Martin dressed in jeans and a light sweater and they drank their tea and wondered how Anna was doing. Then the doorbell rang and Lisa and Martin both looked at each other uncertain of what to do next.

"I'll go answer that, only because my advertising doesn't say I'm now closed for the winter," Martin said as he rose.

Lisa wondered if it was her friend arriving early but at the same time she hoped not. She reached over to the nightstand and picked up her book and started to read. She heard voices getting nearer and was just putting the bookmark back in when Martin came into the room.

"Look who's making a housecall," he said as he stepped aside and their doctor walked in.

"Hi Dr. Brumble," Lisa said.

"Hi Lisa, I was just telling Martin here that I'd missed you on my rounds at the hospital and understand you had quite a bit of excitement yesterday," he said.

Lisa nodded. "A little too much for my liking and I'm not sure I like the prognosis," she replied looking at Martin and smiling.

"Well, I read what had happened and I understand they gave you some meds without even waiting to see what would happen," he said looking to them for confirmation.

Lisa nodded and he nodded back.

After scratching his chin for a moment he looked at them both. "Do you mind if I examine Lisa?" he asked, his eyes resting on hers.

Lisa shook her head. "Not at all, why?" she asked.

Martin stepped to the other side of the bed as the doctor began removing pillows, all but one, from behind Lisa. "I need you to lie down," he said gently.

Lisa pushed herself down and let the doctor begin is exam. He started by pressing down slightly on her stomach and then he placed both hands over where he uterus now was. He waited, then when he seemed satisfied with that he took a special unit out of his carry bag that he called a Doppler and placed a little bit of clear sticky stuff on it before he pressed it against her now bare skin. They both heard the heartbeat come to life and Lisa smiled at Martin.

"It's definitely strong," the doctor said as he recorded some of the numbers. "There's also no contraction activity at all," he said. "Have the two of you been intimate?" he asked.

"No," Lisa said first sounding disappointed.

"Not at all?" the doctor asked.

"A little," Martin admitted. "We wanted to make love but we just got friendly instead."

"That's good," the doctor said.

They both furrowed their brows waiting for him to tell them something, anything but he remained silent as he pulled a pair of gloves from his bag, put them on followed by some clear goop. "I want to finish my exam," he told Lisa who nodded.

She pulled her legs up the way she'd been shown in the hospital and let him finish the exam.

He snapped the gloves off and smiled. "I think what happened was just a freak thing. You were under stress and I think you just got a little winded. I also think you started to have some Braxton-Hicks contractions at the same time and rather than waiting to see if it would pass, they jumped the gun and started the IV," he explained. He went on to explain what those types of contractions were.

"So, the drugs didn't really do anything?" Lisa asked.

"No, they won't hurt you or the baby, but they weren't necessary either," he replied. "You should continue on like nothing happened. If something *does* happen, which I feel is *highly* unlikely, then give me a call and I'll see you at that time. When I say *highly* I'm speaking with almost 100% certainty."

Martin and Lisa smiled at each other. "Then all of this was a waste?" he asked.

"I'm sorry to say that it was," the doctor replied. "I'm sorry I wasn't there, I would have warded off your concerns right from the start."

"But what about the doctor at the hospital?"

"Erring on the side of caution because she didn't know you or your history Lisa," the doctor explained. "I know you kids are getting married tomorrow and I'm just really sorry that this had to happen to interrupt. But go on, get up, shower, have a bath, make love, get married."

Martin walked him to the door, still in a fair bit of shock. He shook the doctor's hand. "Thank you so much," he said.

"You're welcome Martin. I had to see how she was doing," he said. "I also had to provide some answers."

"We'll be eternally grateful. Won't you please come tomorrow," Martin invited.

"I wouldn't miss it," the doctor replied. "And I didn't do this just so you can have sex."

Martin looked at him slyly. "I don't want to just have sex," he said.

The doctor looked at him and smiled. "I don't know about the two of you but I knew that. Just be a little careful." With that, he left and went to his car while Martin watched after him and gave him a wave. He took the stairs two at a time and was shocked when he found Lisa naked, waiting for him. He stopped in the doorway. "Didn't take you long," he said as he stared at her. She was so damn beautiful and he sighed but got undressed and went to her. He wrapped his arms around her and kissed her. He held her breast, then kissed her there. He finally began caressing her and as she climaxed at his touch, he felt so much tension come out of her, he didn't know how she had carried it all on her shoulders alone. He moved above her and slid himself inside her and they both let out sighs. Exasperation, finality had reached them, bringing their need to new heights.

After, they lay side by side, Martin not letting go of her. Whispering in her ear, reminding her that by the end of the next day, she would be his wife, he smiled at her giggling as he did so.

"Can we take a walk?" Lisa asked. "I feel like I've been cooped up forever."

"I think you have been, let's go," he replied.

He went downstairs first and made a thermos of hot chocolate and got their coats ready.

Lisa came down and slid into her coat and boots before she pulled on earmuffs with her hood over top and a heavy pair of mittens.

Martin kissed her cheek and zipped up his own coat before he pulled on his heavy gloves and grabbed the thermos. He held it out to her to show her.

"Smells yummy," she said and smiled. She was only a little angry that the hospital staff had been so quick to treat something she hadn't actually had and she said so on the way down to the beach.

"Yeah especially since we weren't allowed to have sex," Martin replied trying to lighten the mood a little.

"It wasn't just that though," Lisa said.

"I know, I was teasing," Martin replied. "I *do* understand what you're trying to say. They were too quick to diagnose and treat a non-existent problem and it caused you an unnecessary amount of grief that you didn't need three days before our wedding."

Lisa nodded. She was glad he was able to put that into words for her because it made her realize he was fully aware of her feelings which made her feel better and made her love him even more.

They held hands, shared some of the hot chocolate and then raced back to the house, where they took their coats and boots off before racing upstairs and making love before Martin filled the tub so Lisa could get in and warm up. He went downstairs and made some lunch and he served her there in the tub, trying desperately to keep his hands to himself.

Finally, she got out and towelled off. She was getting dressed when she heard the doorbell ring and realized it was probably her friend just arriving. She listened closely and finally heard Jenny's voice echoing up from the foyer, then she heard Martin telling her to follow him and he'd show her to her room. They had decided they would give her the room closest to theirs and make like all the rest were a little better for when her parents arrived. She certainly didn't want them *that* close to her even though she wouldn't be spending the night in the house with them.

Lisa met them at the top of the stairs and Jenny pulled her into her arms. "Oh my God, I can't believe you're getting married tomorrow," she exclaimed.

Lisa laughed. "I can't believe that it's finally here but I'm so glad you could come," she replied.

"I wouldn't have missed it for the world," Jenny said. "And if I had, I wouldn't have believed you'd actually done it," she added as she nudged Martin.

He laughed along but wasn't sure what she meant by that.

"So what have you two been up to?" she asked. "Okay, I know, you're pregnant so it's obvious you've been doing *that*," she went on.

They all laughed with that observation as Jenny reached out and placed her hands on Lisa's tiny bulge.

"You're starting to show already," she commented.

Lisa nodded, "if you wait long enough, you may feel the baby kick too."

Jenny got quiet and held her hands there but felt nothing. "Guess it's asleep."

Lisa shrugged her shoulders. "Have you seen your room yet?" she asked. She suddenly realized she really wasn't prepared for Jenny's arrival, especially the never-ending chatter.

"No, I haven't, Martin was just about to show me though," she replied.

"Yes, it's right through here," he said, grateful he was able to put her bags down finally.

"It's gorgeous," Jenny commented as she followed him in. She called out to Lisa. "Come help me unpack and chat with me," she said.

Lisa shrugged at Martin and he kissed her as he passed her in the doorway. She sat on the bed as Jenny started to unpack and filled her in on everything that had been going on. She told her how she'd come to this place in the first place and the instant connection she'd felt to Martin. She went on about the ghost and the attic and told her all about Sophia and Anna.

Jenny was amazed by the story and couldn't blame Lisa at all for having made the choice she had. "You made the perfect decision."

"I'm glad someone thinks so. My mother's going to be the most annoying tomorrow, I can just feel it," Lisa said.

"Don't worry about it," Jenny said.

Martin had managed to make supper in the time it took and he called them to the dining room.

They all chatted easily through supper and talked about the wedding the following day as well as the rehearsal they'd soon be attending.

The rest of the evening went smoothly and they all retired early, Martin making love to Lisa once again before he pulled her into his arms knowing that the following night when he did this, he would be holding his wife in his arms and he smiled and fell asleep with that smile on his face.

CHAPTER 21

The day of the wedding was sunny and dry. Lisa left with Jenny around mid-morning to go into town where they picked up their dresses and went to get their hair done at the local salon. Anna had insisted that Lisa wear Sophia's headpiece so perhaps it could see a happier union. It went perfectly with the gown she'd picked out so she'd agreed. She'd had to get the veil replaced as it had been moth-eaten but it gave her the opportunity to have colours matched as her gown was not the traditional white. The tiara was crystal and pearl and was in great condition.

Jenny and Lisa chatted endlessly, still trying to catch up with everything that had happened in the last five months, and Jenny was still so enthralled with Lisa's story about her chance meeting with Martin and more so with the story of Sophia that she couldn't resist asking questions that even Lisa didn't know the answer to.

The hairdresser was also taken with the story as she'd heard the rumours often but, like everyone else, never fully believed them.

Soon after, they thanked the staff profusely and left. Jenny complimented Lisa repeatedly on her hair and headpiece as they sped back to the house, where Martin had left lunch for them before he had left with his best man for a late lunch, a stop at the barber and then on to the church where he would get dressed and be waiting at the altar for her.

It wasn't long after they ate and finished getting dressed that Lisa's family arrived followed by the photographer who took an endless number of pictures of the decorated house while waiting for them all to finish getting ready to go.

Lisa's mother started complaining right away about Lisa and her choices. "I think the house is beautiful but too small for the wedding reception. It's going to get far too warm..."

"Knock it off mom or leave, it's *my* wedding."

After that, there was an obvious tension between the two but Lisa was glad she'd made the choice she had. She'd been concerned about her mother not wanting her to move so far away but after this display, she didn't care. She smiled even bigger and brighter for her photos and the ones of her with her family were definitely tense. The little kids were dressed and looking gorgeous and ready to take on their duties as flower girls.

Lisa was only shocked for a few moments when the doorbell rang and it was answered to a limo driver. She smiled, realizing that Martin must have taken care of this little detail while she wasn't around.

"Let's go everyone," she announced and everyone put their coats on before they went outside. Lisa was the last to go and the driver, John, took extra special care with her gown.

She settled into the back of the limo and closed her eyes for a moment only to open them to find her mother with somewhat of a scowl on her face. "What did I do now mother?" she asked.

Her mother was a little shocked and she fumbled before she finally said nothing and that it was very kind of Martin to think of the limousine.

It wasn't a long drive but felt like an eternity to Lisa who felt her stomach turn over once in anticipation as they pulled up in front of the old building. Then she felt the baby kick and her hand went to her stomach out of reflex. She took it away as soon as she realized that she hadn't told her mother she was pregnant and she wasn't sure how she was going to break that news when the baby was born. She forgot about it as everyone was ushered out of the car and went inside the church and then John came back for her. She took a deep breath, smiled at him and lifted herself out. He helped her inside and waited for the appropriate music to start playing before he took hold of her train and as she started walking let go so it fell behind her as perfectly as it should have been. She was walking down the aisle alone as she'd felt it inappropriate for her father to give her away. She'd been living with Martin, and after discussing it with her father, had chosen to do this on her own.

She reached Martin, who held a hand out for her and she slid hers inside.

The minister began the service in the usual fashion and before long reached the exchange of vows.

Martin looked at Lisa and knew what he wanted to say right from the start. "Lisa, you walked into my life and into my heart in the same moment. I fell in love with you before even I knew what was happening. I feared you wouldn't think twice because of the years between us, but you have surprised us both I think," he stopped and smiled at her. "I have waited for this moment since that first day, the moment when I can tell you, in front of all our friends and family, how much I love you and promise that I will love you and cherish you for all the days of my life."

Lisa had to look up to the ceiling to keep the tears from streaming down her cheeks. "Martin, I can't say how much I love you because there are no words to say it. But when I walked into your life, I felt as though I'd been there all my life. You have changed my life and made me dreams real. For that, I will love you now and for all the days of my life, carry you in my heart."

Martin too had tears in his eyes and he was told he could kiss the bride and he took Lisa into his arms with a passion he'd been holding back since she'd walked down the aisle and had slid her hand into his own.

They exchanged rings and went off to sign the register before they were pronounced husband and wife and walked down the aisle together. They ran straight out to the limo and sped off as they'd had no intentions of having a receiving line at the church. They needed to get back to the house ahead of everyone else.

When they had arrived, Martin thanked the driver profusely and gave him an extra large tip before he led Lisa inside and locked the door for a few moments.

"You look absolutely delectable," he told her. "And I love the gown," he said of the gold topped gown she'd chosen for the occasion with a full, off-white tulle skirt.

"Thank you. You don't look half bad yourself with your little ascot," she replied as she pressed her hand against the multi-coloured silk.

He kissed her long and hard. "I can't wait until tonight," he whispered.

"Neither can I," she whispered back.

"How are you feeling?" he asked, serious now.

"I'm okay. Tired though."

"Why don't you go upstairs, I'll hold off the well-wishers and tell them you went to freshen up. Just sit, or lie down for a few minutes."

Lisa nodded. "I'll do that. Thank you."

She kissed him before she lifted her skirt and made her way carefully up the stairs. She reached the landing just as the doorbell rang to announce her family's return and her brother and brother-in-law quickly took over answering the door and ushering people towards the dining room.

Martin had managed to escape from the throng of people waiting to shake his hand or hung him and wish him well. He went upstairs where he found Lisa sitting in one of the chairs by the window watching outside and he went to her and sank down onto his knees before her. "I want to make love to you right now," he told her.

"I wish we hadn't planned a reception because I'd love to just crawl into bed right now and have you make love to me before I drift off to sleep."

Martin smiled up at her before he rose on his knees and kissed her. He leaned back and looked at her.

"What are you staring at?" she asked.

"You. Just how beautiful you are, how you amaze me," he replied.

She smiled. "I love you."

They spoke quietly for a few more moments before she, with Martin's help, got out of the chair and, bypassing their pre-packed bags, went into the bathroom.

Just as she closed the door, Lisa's brother came up and told Martin the photographer was looking for the bride and groom for some pictures.

"She *just* went into the bathroom. We'll be right down. I'm just going to make sure she doesn't fall in with that whole crinoline thing she's got going on," Martin replied, teasing.

Steven laughed. "Yeah, women," he said and went back downstairs.

Lisa came out not long after and Martin told her what her brother had said. She retreated back into the bathroom just to fix her makeup before allowing Martin to lead her downstairs.

The photographer waved them into the den where he posed them both alone, and got some very intimate pictures of the two of them before he proceeded to calling in the wedding party and her family.

Lisa found herself getting more and more tired and wasn't sure how long she was going to last without a bit of a break.

Just as she thought that, the photographer said he'd had enough with the bride and she gave Jenny a knowing look and disappeared quietly back upstairs. This time she took her shoes off, flung her gown up onto the bed and lay down for a while. It felt wonderful to be able to be flat on her back and close her eyes. Of course that was when the baby started kicking and she smiled as she laid a hand over her tummy and just felt the small kicks. Soon she drifted off.

"You looked beautiful today my dear," the voice said. Lisa was looking this way and that and she finally realized she was outside in the backyard and she looked up at the house. She saw Sophia standing there and gave a little wave.

"Thank you," Lisa replied looking down at her gown.

"No, thank you," Sophia said. "You reunited me with my daughter and for that I will be forever grateful. I can't wait to meet her."

"She has been a delight to have in my life."

"I wish you all the best with your own children," Sophia told her.

"Thank you."

"I will be leaving you now," Sophia said.

"I'm going to miss you, sort of," Lisa replied with a small chuckle.

Sophia was smiling down at her. *"I will kind of miss being here too but I have my own child to get to know now too."*

"I hope she doesn't go too soon," Lisa replied. *"I'd like for her to meet my baby."*

"If she can't, we'll both be watching over you and we'll meet her anyway."

Lisa felt tears in her eyes. She knew that in some small way it was a hint of what was to come.

"Goodbye, and say goodbye to Martin too. He's a wonderful man, cherish him for as long as you can."

"He's so very special to me, I want to make as many memories as I can so I have them for when he's gone," Lisa replied.

Sophia nodded. *"He'll stand by you,"* she said wistfully.

Lisa understood so much about Sophia. *"I know. He's different."*

"Yes, he is."

They said goodbye and Lisa was left standing in the yard by herself but now someone else was calling to her. *"Lisa."*

She woke to Martin's voice. She opened her eyes to find him looking at her.

"You okay?" he asked.

Lisa nodded. "Sophia is leaving us and so will Anna be, soon."

Martin nodded. "We knew that."

"I know but I really wanted her to be able to hold our baby first," Lisa replied.

Martin held her. "Did you have a good sleep? How are you feeling?" he asked.

"I did, and I'm feeling better. Not as tired."

He helped her up to sitting and then on with her shoes before he got her up off the bed. "Good because it's dinner time," he told her.

He led her downstairs and Lisa would never be sure if he'd planned it but they rounded the banister and were walking into the dining room at the same time their MC was announcing them. Everyone clapped as they made their way the head table and before long the caterers were putting platters of food on the table.

Everyone was in great spirits and it wasn't long before they were eating dessert, and the MC started the speeches. When it was Martin's turn to stand up and make a toast to his bride, he announced to the room that they were expecting a baby in the spring.

Lisa looked to where her mother was sitting and almost fell off her chair. Her mother was actually smiling. She couldn't believe it. She was completely shocked. After, she learned that her mother thought she was making a mistake because she assumed Martin couldn't have children. Lisa set her straight on a number of things, including that Martin had been married young but his wife had gotten breast cancer before they could ever have children. He had then gone on to life as usual as it could be without them and didn't think he would ever find anyone else, after she died a few years before, until Lisa had walked into his life. Her mother had made amends, the best she could on short notice, and told her they were welcome anytime and could stay with them for however long.

Lisa's smile was truly genuine while they were cutting the cake and celebrating their first dance as husband and wife as everyone looked on, camera flashes everywhere they turned.

A few hours later Martin and Lisa were in the car, the trunk packed with their things and they were heading towards Bayfield. Lisa had said goodbye to her parents which included a slew of 'I'm sorry's' from her mom. Lisa reminded her mom she soon wouldn't be able to travel and her mother told her there was always the phone and that she would be delighted to come up and stay a while after the baby was born. Lisa had a lot to absorb. She had cried finally, all over her mother, and later Martin, at how things had ended up.

"I told you they would eventually," Martin told her.

"I know but sometimes life throws a curve and you never know," she replied cryptically.

Well, we have to keep that in mind always don't we?"

When they arrived in Bayfield, Maria wanted to sit them down and hear all about the wedding and Martin had to remind her that Lisa was expecting and that she'd had a very long day and was very tired.

"In the morning then," she told them. "Over a huge breakfast."

Martin and Lisa nodded and climbed the stairs to their favourite room. Maria was keeping it almost solely for them now and they went inside where they made love.

"You are my wife," Martin said as he entered her.

"And you are my husband," Lisa replied.

They got lost after that and each cried out 'I love you,' at the appropriate time. They fell asleep, content they'd made it through the day with dreams of their future and their baby.

EPILOGUE

The day had started bright and for the first time in a month, Lisa had been energetic enough to go down to the beach and walk through the sand. It was four days past her due date and she was reflecting on the four months since their wedding. They'd had a huge birthday party for Anna at the home and surprised her. They had visited often and she was always feeling Lisa's tummy for kicks.

It was late at night in the middle of May when they'd gotten the phone call from the home that Anna had been taken to the hospital. They were told it wasn't serious so they had gone back to sleep only to wake in the morning to another phone call telling them that Anna wasn't doing well but she was asking for them. They had raced to the hospital where she had spoken to them quite lucidly, surprising all of the staff. She'd told Lisa to take care of her baby and she'd told Martin to take good care of his family. They'd both nodded, tears welling up in their eyes as she held both their hands and it was when they'd finally said goodbye and Lisa had pressed Anna's hand against her stomach that Anna had smiled and as the baby gave a kick, Anna's breathing stopped and the line on her heart monitor went to a flat line.

Martin had pulled Lisa into his arms and held her tight while she cried and the staff moved about them to quiet the machines and the doctor pronounced her death.

They had gone to the small, quiet funeral and Lisa had been mourning her ever since.

Now it was a month later and Lisa finally went to the beach where she'd sorted through so many of her thoughts when she'd first arrived. She'd settled herself down after the funeral and chose a few items of Anna's that she wanted to keep. Everything Anna had taken that was Sophia's came back to the house as well.

She felt a twinge as she walked along and thought it was the baby kicking again but when she touched her stomach it was hard. She thought it was another Braxton-Hicks contraction but then she felt a stabbing pain in her back and started to wonder differently. She hurried back to the stairs and called Martin's name. She had to stop at the bottom of the stairs and looked upwards. She began the climb to the top and Martin appeared when she had reached the small landing, halfway up.

"Are you okay?" he asked.

Lisa shook her head. "I don't think so. I think labour has started," she told him.

He rushed down the stairs and took her arm to help her to the top. He sat her in one of the chairs there and watched her. "How many?" he asked.

"Just one so far," she told him.

"What were you thinking, going down to the beach four days after your due date?" he scolded.

"I finally had the energy to do it," she told him.

Then another contraction hit and she held onto the arms of the chair. "Yep, I think this is the real thing," she said.

Martin checked his watch to start timing them and got her out of the chair as soon as it was over and into the house.

He went upstairs after he sat her in a chair in the den but when he came back down she was in the kitchen leaning on the breakfast bar. He looked again at his watch and realized her contractions were about seven minutes apart. "I have your things," he told her. "Are you ready to go?"

She nodded as she breathed through the pain and let him lead her to the front door and out to the car.

They chatted on the way to the hospital, stopping intermittently for Lisa to let a contraction pass as she grabbed Martin's hand.

It was several hours later when the doctor was finally telling Lisa to push.

"I'm too tired," she said to Martin.

"You need to push Lisa, it's the baby, it's coming out," Martin told her.

The doctor gave an encouraging word and Lisa began pushing.

"It's a girl!" the doctor announced. He continued to work after he had put the baby on Lisa's stomach and the nurses were hovering around cleaning off the baby.

When the doctor had cut the cord, the nurses took the baby to be weighed and measured as Lisa gave a squeal of annoyance.

"They're weighing her," Martin whispered in her ear.

"Oh," she replied.

The doctor finished and let the nursing staff take over from there.

They brought the baby back and handed her to her mother. The baby started to cry so they helped her to get the baby latched onto her breast.

Lisa smiled. It felt awkward at first but once she got used to it and the baby was doing well, it didn't feel so bad. She looked up at Martin who was smiling down at her, watching his daughter eating for the first time.

"So, what are you going to name her?" one of the nurses asked.

"We're going to name her Anna Sophia, after some very dear friends of ours," Lisa replied looking up at Martin who nodded his approval.

A few weeks later, when they had settled into a routine, Lisa and Martin took Anna to see her namesakes' grave so that Anna could see the baby though they both knew Anna would have already checked in with them. Lisa cried as she had so wanted Anna to be able to hold the baby and be at her christening but like all things, it didn't seem to work out that way.

Martin held her and reminded her of what Sophia had told her in the dream. Then he held her for a few moments. "Do you want to know something?" he asked.

Lisa looked up at him, tears glistening in the sunlight, and nodded.

"Our daughter was born exactly four months after our wedding."

Lisa looked at him, then she counted and realized he was right. She'd been born June sixteenth.

They gave one last look at Anna's headstone with the angel on it and walked down the path, hand in hand to continue on their journey together.

Pamela lives in Waterloo, ON, Canada with her daughter Sam. She is the author of *To Love Again, At Sunset, Let The Dream Begin, Til We Meet Again, and The Journey Home.* Besides writing, she enjoys swimming, reading and movies. She's heavily involved at church including singing in the choir. *Mystery in the Attic* is her sixth published novel and there are many more to come.

For more information, visit her on the web at www.lulu.com/worksbyplc or www.freewebs.com/worksbyplc

Other Titles:

To Love Again

Michelle is a single mom hurt by a tough marriage that ended
abruptly. She thinks she can never trust another man until
she meets Greg—who falls in love with her at first sight.
Eventually Michelle gives in to Greg's pursuits when she
realizes his only 'agenda' is to lover her and her daughter.
As love finally blossoms between the two, Michelle's past
resurfaces threatening to harm her and, possibly, destroy her
newfound faith and love.

At Sunset

Angie is a hardworking lawyer with a busy practice. She
doesn't have time for dating and doesn't believe in love at
first sight or soulmates.
Then David walks into her office and there's an instant
connection that neither can understand.
Angie tries to run away only to be drawn back by a power
beyond her control.
When they turn to their faith for answers, they discover that
love *can* triumph.

Let The Dream Begin

Lucy Everett is new to the stage, love... and life, but not to
music. In fact music is the one constant in her life.
When she steps on the stage for the first time, she doesn't
just fall in love with performing, she also falls for Michael
Corway, the director of this amateur production of Phantom
Of The Opera. She suddenly feels a connection deeper than
she has ever known or can understand.
With a supportive best friend, and a crew that adopts her into
their theatrical family by her side, Lucy learns about the
stage, life... and love.

Til We Meet Again

Katie's just moved to town after inheriting her late grandmother's house. She has a new job and a new man in her life.

But soon after she starts dating Dean, she starts having vivid dreams that leave her confused and searching for answers. As the pieces of the puzzle are discovered they uncover a heart-wrenching, tragic love affair that's closer to home than she could have imagined.

The Journey Home

Sophie's in danger and running away from the East Coast, and her past, with no destination in mind. Her ex-boss is able to help and she gratefully finds refuge wtih Henry in Southwestern Ontario.

She's torn by new, intense feelings and whether she should be having these feelings--according to one counsellor she shouldn't be.

But despite that, she turns to her intuition and a good friend she met along the way and starts on a new journey.